I0597253

AUDIO ASSAULT

CODENAME: WINGER #3

JEFF ADAMS

AUDIO ASSAULT

CODENAME: WINGER #3

JEFF ADAMS

PRAISE FOR
CODENΔME: WINGER

"A fun and intriguing adventure with fast-paced action and a delightfully authentic voice in Theo. Part mystery, part thriller, and all heart."

TJ KLUNE, NEW YORK TIMES
BESTSELLING AUTHOR OF *THE
EXTRAORDINARIES*

"An unforgettable thrill ride! Equal parts smart and suspenseful."

JULIAN WINTERS, AWARD-WINNING
AUTHOR OF *RUNNING WITH LIONS*

"Theo is a sixteen-year-old junior in high school, a tech whiz, and a swoonable cocktail of sweet and tough. He's exactly the kind of character I want to read about."

GREGORY ASHE, AUTHOR OF THE
HOLLOW FOLK SERIES

ONE

"Winger, Amp here. My position's about to be compromised. I'm not sure how much longer I can stay here."

Through the comm channel, tension dripped from the agent's quiet voice. Twenty-three years old and new to Tactical Operational Support, Amp sounded green and unsure. Reminded me of my first field mission less than a year ago.

"Hang tight, Amp. Focus on the neutralization of the firewall." I projected calm because it's what my team needed. Meanwhile, from an electrical equipment closet on the first floor, I worked to take over the research facility's security system so it would appear as though multiple breaches were in progress. "Petty, do you have eyes on Amp's position?"

"There are three working to open the door where Amp is." Petty didn't have a tremble in her voice even though this was her first time too. No doubt part of that was her safer position in the van outside. *"They've brought in a blowtorch to get through the door."*

"Winger, what am I going to do?"

"You keep working. You're there because you know what needs to be done. We'll keep you safe."

The building's security was ridiculous in its complexity. Usually it was easy to find the logic in a system, this one seemed to have none. Maybe that was the point. I hoped to use the intricacies to force its downfall.

"Petty, how many inside?"

"*Stand by.*"

As the seconds ticked by, I got fidgety. "Petty?"

"*Winger, one moment.*"

"Don't have a moment, Petty." Annoyance slipped into my voice, which I didn't like. Petty and Amp were assigned to me for this mission, and it fell to me to be senior agent in charge.

"*Winger, they're cutting through. There's already a small hole in the door. I need at least another two minutes.*"

"Understood, Amp." He was right on schedule. In the mission briefing, he said he'd need fifteen minutes, and he was at thirteen. "Petty, now."

"*Seventeen across the three floors. Biggest clusters are on three and one.*"

Time to make a distraction. I sent commands to deceive the security system into thinking an intruder breached a second-floor lab.

"Petty, disable the monitors on my mark but maintain your visibility."

"*Understood. Standing by.*"

After a double-check of the commands, I poised my finger over the enter key. "Now, Petty."

"*Monitors disabled.*"

"Distraction enabled." The security statuses flipped from green to red on the south side of the second floor.

"*No one's moving to that area, Winger.*"

"What?"

"Confirmed." Petty continued. *"They're ignoring it."*

What the hell? My monitor returned to green status. Everything seemed in order to make this work, especially since I saw—There was a loop of logic checks. This design was clever. I read quickly through the code and found the subroutine causing the problem.

"Stand by."

We got bad intel on this place. No mention of buried security measures appeared in any of the reports. If we'd known that, we wouldn't have sent Amp in before we knew we had control. I shouldn't have sent him to start before I confirmed we could keep him safe. Now we needed an improvised distraction or he'd be exposed and the mission would fail.

I typed rapidly, looking for a way to make the security sensors trip.

"Petty, keep me posted on Amp's status."

"Copy that, Winger."

Nothing worked. Apparently only the door sensor could send the right command back to central control to confirm an intruder. There was no time to figure this out.

"Damnit. Winger, I need more time. I've run into interference. Someone's trying to kick me out. My timeline is shot."

"Understood, Amp. Petty, do you have eyes on me?"

"Confirmed, Winger."

This sucked hard, but there was little choice. If I couldn't make a distraction remotely, I'd have to do it manually.

"Amp, I'm en route to your location. Keep at it and stop for nothing."

"But—"

"Understood?"

Silence filled the channel for a moment. *"Copy that."* He clearly didn't like it.

"Petty, help me stay out of sight."

"Got it. You're clear for the corridor you're in and then on to the elevators and stairs."

"Understood."

Despite the info, I opened the door slowly and peeked around the corner. Since it was after hours, the lighting was at half, but that wouldn't obscure me if anyone came into the hall.

Amp was on the second floor, but I wanted a distraction down here to draw people in this direction. The windows would be a good target if I could disrupt those sensors. I pulled my phone as I got to the stairs and brought up the building schematics. I needed to know where the sensors were.

"Winger," Petty said. *"Guards leaving the lobby. Get out of the hall."*

I opened the stairway door slowly to avoid noise and ducked in. There was no window in the door so I couldn't see once it closed.

"Stand by. They're past you but not out of the hall."

All the doors and windows had sensors. I looked around the perimeter of the stairwell door and found one along the top.

Damn. No wires ran to the small block so severing the connection couldn't happen. There was no time to figure out how to disrupt the wireless network that linked the sensors.

New plan.

I considered my options as I sprinted upstairs.

"Petty, tell me about the third floor."

4

"Two guards are at the elevator bank behind a desk. Another is on patrol. Exit the staircase, go right and then left, and you'll be out of sight for a few moments. But you've got to move now."

I moved quick, happy I kept up with endurance exercises during the hockey off-season. At the door, I asked, "Clear?"

"Clear."

I ended up in a hall filled with doors locked by retinal-scan and card-access readers. This should do the trick.

"Amp here. I think I've got less than five minutes before they're in here. There's even more resistance in the network. They're tag-teaming me. I could really use you in here, Winger."

"Here comes the distraction."

I stepped up to the first scanner and pushed the only available button. Bright light hit my eye and the scanner turned red.

"Unauthorized," a mechanical female voice announced.

Finally.

I moved to the next door and did it again.

"Three guards are headed your way."

I moved to the other scanners quickly. The more alerts the better.

"Petty, next stairwell?"

"Three doors down on your left. You've got maybe fifteen seconds before they'll see you."

I ignored other sensors and made for the staircase.

"Where am I going to come out on two?" I asked as I headed down.

Another set of labs, bigger. Only two on the corridor. The guards are checking the doors on three, but one is headed into the stairway, and he's on his radio.

"Which way do I go to get to Amp?"

"Out of the staircase, go right. That's clear. Finding the best route from there."

"Copy that."

I followed the instructions and pressed my eye into the sensors at the labs I passed.

"You don't have time for that. Take the next right and then look sharp. There are a lot of intersections. You're going to take the third left, and you'll be in the corridor where Amp is. He's still got one person on his door. The other guards have dispersed, most are on three."

I jogged down the hall with a stop to scan my unauthorized eye. Unexpectedly the hall lights went red and klaxons sounded.

That was new. Even though I didn't know what caused it, I appreciated the extra noise to bring attention here.

"Amp's door is clear. The guard's coming your way. Two more from behind. Get to the last intersection and go left. That's the clearest bet, and you'll get back to Amp."

This was more fun than it should be. Sure, bad guys were coming, but running around in the corridors was an ultimate game of laser tag. I desperately did not want to get tagged.

"Winger, I'm in." I smiled at the thrill in Amp's voice. *"Beginning data transfer."*

"Excellent. I'm on my way. Less than a minute."

"You need to hurry, Winger. The guards are all responding to the last alarm you triggered. Take the next right. Amp is two doors from the end of the corridor. They'll cut you off if you don't hurry."

I didn't have much speed to add, but I pushed.

"The guy's back working with the door." Petty broke the news just as I turned into the hallway. We were both

dressed in black. Maybe he'd mistake me for security as well.

"He's almost through the entire frame." To his credit, Amp sounded calmer.

I slowed. The man at the door needed to believe I was part of his team.

"Winger, you're about to get pinned if the guard in the staircase to your left enters the floor."

There was nowhere for me to go.

"Amp," I was very quiet, knowing the comms would still pick up my voice, "no matter what finish the mission and make sure you get all the data."

There was only a short pause. *"Understood."*

I heard the stairway open behind me and boots on the floor.

"You there," barked a new voice, "identify yourself."

"Security. Hauer." I didn't turn or break stride.

He's closing on you, Winger.

The loud clomps made that obvious. He must not have a stealth mode. The dude at the door turned his attention to me.

"Amp, can you help Winger?"

"No. The download is too unstable."

"Where's your badge?" asked the guy who'd been cutting the door open. A badge clipped to the front of his shirt hung over the pocket. He dropped his hand to the holster at his waist.

"Oh, man. Sorry. I forgot to clip it on when I started my shift." Fishing around in my pockets, I had to buy a few more seconds.

"I've never heard of a Hauer," said the man behind me. He shoved me forward as the guy in front of me aimed his gun. "Get your hands out of your pockets."

When I didn't immediately comply, he grabbed my right hand to forcibly remove it.

"Who are you? How'd you get in here?" Another shove from behind sent me sideways into the wall.

"I'll have to talk to HR if you keep touching me." I shrugged him off as he grabbed for me. "I told you I've got a badge. I just need to get it."

"Winger, what are you doing?" Petty sounded nervous.

"Let me help you." The man was in my face and he dug into my left pocket but came up with nothing. From my right, he pulled out my phone. "He's got no ID." He threw the phone to the floor.

"Now, who are you?" The man with the gun asked as he moved closer.

"Hey, Siri. Pulse."

"Opening app Pulse," Siri said.

"What did you do?"

"Five...." A male voice came from the phone.

"Turn it off." The man with the gun twitched as the other guard picked up the phone.

"Four...."

He pulled the gun's hammer back. "Now."

"Three...."

"Hey, Siri. Stop Pulse!" the guard clutched the phone, screaming at it.

Did he really think it would take commands from anyone but me?

"Two...."

"Stop it!" the gunman shouted at me, but I only shook my head. "Smash it!"

The guy holding the phone threw it down and stomped on it with his heel.

"One...." Despite the crunch of the screen's glass, it kept going.

The gun fired.

The impact slammed my chest.

"Pulse."

Sparks flew from the lights and door mechanisms as well as the guard's pockets.

I clutched my chest where the bullet hit.

"Winger!" Amp and Petty shouted into my ear.

Pain radiated from my chest as I crumpled to the floor.

Both guards shook, and one cried out, as they fell.

"Get that data secured," I called out as red spilled out between my fingers.

"MISSION ACCOMPLISHED. Target data acquired. Two TOS agents in the clear. One TOS agent dead. Two enemy agents incapacitated. One enemy agent dead." The female voice echoed through the corridors of the building.

With the exercise completed, I could get up. Numbness pulsed in my left arm because of the way I fell. Since dead guys don't move, I couldn't shift my position.

The two guards I'd taken out—the ones reported as incapacitated stirred as well. The three of us groaned in unison.

"I can't believe you shot me. You know how that feels." I glared and grinned simultaneously at Zan, who sat with one leg bent and his other out in front of him. I stood and offered him a hand up.

"You zapped us. What was I supposed to do? Go down quietly?"

"Well, if Leonardo here hadn't kept my phone, I would've been just as fried as you two."

"Sure, blame it on me. Next time, the phone goes out of Siri's hearing range."

That gave me an idea for an enhancement. Siri needed to be tied into the comms so if the phone was out of range—whether deliberate or accidental—the agent could still access the commands that we'd made Siri-friendly.

Siri proved to be a valuable addition to our arsenal of gadgets—easy to integrate with so we didn't have to build our own solution but flexible enough we could make it secure for our use. It was a blast to work on Siri additions, like Pulse, which also required an upgrade to the phone itself to allow for the energy discharge.

"Do you have any idea the bruise I'll have from the shot? The Kevlar only—"

"Oh my God, Theo!" I smiled at Petty, who ran down the hall toward me. "I'm glad you're okay. I had no idea this was a simulation."

"You weren't supposed to." I grinned. "You did good, Sarina. Where's Darnell?" In all the people streaming into the hallway, I didn't see him.

"He's... a little shaken." She appeared sheepish. I cocked my head and raised an eyebrow. "He's in the bathroom downstairs. Sounded like he might be sick."

I nodded. "I'll go check on him. We'll debrief at HQ at one." I turned and pointed to Zan. "You owe me at least a case of Dr Pepper. I'll see you guys later."

I left to find Darnell. A few people along the way stopped me to chat about the simulation or congratulate me on the job we'd done. I didn't know the success rate on this one but planned to check before the briefing to see how we measured up.

I found Darnell gripping the sides of the sink as the water ran. He stared into the basin.

"Hey. You okay?" I stepped close but not too close. "You did good. Mission accomplished."

"Coming out of that room... seeing you...." His voice cracked on nearly each word. "I shot somebody." As he looked at me in the reflection of the mirror, his haunted expression indicated his distress. "What if this had been real?"

"Then you did what you needed to do finish the mission and get out." I tossed aside my previous strategy and stepped close to put a hand on his shoulder. "This simulation focuses on how to cope with the stress of a field mission."

Darnell straightened and I moved back. "I may not be cut out for this."

"Maybe. Or it could be the shock of the first time. There's a lot of discussion and analysis to come. We'll sort it out. Not all of us are made for the field and we don't all have to be."

"I'm sorry."

"Don't be. You did good and these reactions are okay."

"Did you know this was a simulation?"

I nodded. "I knew there'd be one, but I didn't know the scenario. Lorenzo threw a curveball with what he did to the security system to force me into the building."

I tried to keep things light so he wouldn't be harder on himself. I knew how difficult missions could be, and I hadn't had the benefit of training like this my first time out.

He nodded, and I made a mental note to flag him for additional counseling. Sarina and Darnell would both get psych reviews to check on their mental state following the exercise, but I'd have to report this because he may be right about not being fit for the field.

"Come on. Let's get some lunch before we spend the afternoon talking about this." Another sullen nod. "And trust me when I say that your reactions are all okay. I've been out on missions twice and it's a lot to process."

He smiled weakly as we walked. "Seems like you do okay."

"You haven't seen me in the immediate aftermath. It's rough out there, but I've learned how to take care of myself, and so will you."

"What if I can't?"

"Like I said, there's plenty to do around here without field certification."

Once again, he nodded and his mood seemed to improve a little.

TWO

Sweat dripped off me as I sprinted to the puck in a race against a hulking defenseman. These pickup games brought out all kinds, and that made them insanely fun. The only consistency, for me at least, was that Mitch and I did this together.

He'd gotten us into roller hockey, and I'd come to appreciate playing in the heat. We were in an ice league for the summer too, which was great, but the contrast of playing the game on pavement proved enjoyable.

I scooped the puck out of reach of the defensemen and crouched low to get by him in a move I wasn't sure I'd be able to execute on ice. The traction of the pavement helped. After taking off toward the opponent's goal, I lined up to shoot, but I saw Mitch get into a good position at the last minute. I passed to him. The goalie hadn't expected the change up, and he left a wide-open net for Mitch to score.

We fist-bumped as we headed back to the sidelines, satisfied with our shift.

"Two minutes left!" called the timekeeper.

With so many playing today, it was unlikely we'd get another shift. At least we went out with a goal.

As we stood with our teammates, I peeled my wet T-shirt off. The roller hockey gear was light, which was good on super-hot July days like this. I grabbed one of the water bottles out of my backpack and drank.

I'd returned from Tactical Operational Support HQ yesterday afternoon just in time to have dinner with Mom and Dad. We were home together for the first time in nearly two months. Then Eddie and I went to the movies, where the latest Marvel movie played while we made out in the back corner of the theater. And this morning was about hockey.

"Jesus, Theo," Mitch said, "I'm still getting used to the angry scar the bullet left, but now this epic bruise. What'd you do?"

"That's from a slap shot." Mitch couldn't take his eyes off the dark, angry splotch that spread from my sternum across part of my right pectoral. "I got invited to a pickup game, and I was able to borrow gear, except the shoulder pads."

That rolled right out of my mouth like it was the truth. I'd used it on Eddie last night, so I was used to saying it.

"Game!" That call rang out and the teams lined up to shake hands. Our team had lost by two and that was okay. Unlike Tigers games, this was purely about fun.

We continued to talk as we gathered our gear. "You need to be more careful. You get hurt way too much. Your parents'll put their foot down eventually."

I laughed as he sounded more like a parent than my friend. If only he knew what my parents actually thought. I'd discussed the training exercise over dinner. My team had performed in the top 10 percent of participants—well beyond expectations for a team of all techs with limited experience. Mom and Dad were proud.

"They're glad this is only a hockey injury."

I pulled out another bottle of water, opened it and poured it over my head. The cool water felt wonderful. Eddie and Iris approached as I toweled off. Even though I'd seen Eddie last night, my heart sped up from the excitement of spending the afternoon with him. There'd been a big empty space in me while I was gone. I hadn't expected to miss him so much. Despite talking and texting daily, it wasn't enough to satisfy my need to be around him.

We planned to spend as much time as possible together this weekend.

"I don't suppose you've got an extra bottle?" Mitch picked up my backpack and looked inside. "Actually, what do you have in here? It weighs a ton. How'd you even bike here with this and a stick on your back?"

I snatched the pack—I didn't like people digging around in there because there were plenty of hidden compartments —and got the last bottle for him. "You know me. I like to be prepared. Besides, if I hadn't brought all this water you'd be dehydrated. And I need a change of clothes."

"If you told me you played without a shirt, I would've come to watch." Eddie wrapped me in a quick hug despite the water and sweat.

"For sure," Iris added. "How often do you get to watch hockey with a bunch of shirtless players? Are you hiding something from me, Mitch?"

Mitch gulped down water before he answered. "You didn't miss anything. Everyone was properly clothed."

Eddie sighed wistfully. "Suppose that's a good thing. This one's getting hurt enough already." He lightly ran his fingers across the bruise, just right so it didn't cause any pain. "Every time he goes away, I fear how he's going to come back."

"Right?" Mitch looked at me and Iris looked at him. "He gets a little more battered every time he leaves town."

"That's not true." I laughed to make light of the situation since they weren't wrong. "The abduction happened right here in Boston."

Iris scowled at me. "Not funny, Theo."

It'd been nearly six months since the computer science tournament, and it seemed like everything had shifted back to normal. School had been out for a month, and so far I'd been away, supposedly working for one of my clients, for just two of those weeks.

I was surprised at everyone's reaction to the bruise because Mitch and I, and the entire hockey team for that matter, got banged up all the time. Maybe it was because this happened while I was gone. I'd stayed in touch while I'd been away, though. Besides Eddie, I texted with Mitch every few days. They should've known I was okay.

"I appreciate the concern, guys, but I've been hurt worse in McKinley games." To help break up the conversation, I toweled off and pulled on a fresh shirt. I got out of the roller hockey pants too, so I was just in shorts. "What's the plan for this afternoon?"

"There's a concert in the park." Iris took out her phone and swiped some screens before passing it to Eddie. "Lots of local bands and food trucks with tons of food. I thought it wouldbe a great way to hang out. Oh, and admission is free."

"Way to keep the best part until last," Mitch said.

"Wow. This is pretty cool," Eddie handed the phone off to me. "I love some of these bands."

"I have no idea about this music, but I'm in. You can't

knock free and close by."

"Exactly. We won't even have to repark the car." Mitch dried off and changed. "We can drop all the stuff in the car and head over. We need to get there soon 'cause I need food."

"See, I thought that's the first thing this one was gonna say." Eddie put his arm around me, and I looked up to roll my eyes at him.

"I'm not even going to debate the need for food with another athlete."

I shoved everything in my backpack, which had more room since the water was gone. Eddie grabbed our sticks, and we headed for Mitch's car. I thought we looked cute walking down the street. Mitch and Iris in front held hands, and Eddie and me followed with our fingers intertwined.

"How can you possibly not know any of the bands?" Iris glanced at me over her shoulder. "I mean, sure, there're a few I haven't heard of, but most of these are played on the local radio stations."

"I don't listen to much music."

"All the time in front of your computer and you don't even have an app open to play music? How's that possible? Eddie, is he serious or does he listen to something weird he wants to hide?"

Eddie looked at me, and I shrugged so he knew he could say whatever. "It's true. And when he does listen, it's usually older stuff. He got most of his musical taste from his parents with a lot of eighties pop, but there's other stuff that I've never heard of."

Iris's mouth hung open in disbelief as we got to the car. "We've got to do something about this. There's such amazing music. You're missing out."

I chuckled. "I don't know. I hear random stuff all the

time that I can't stand."

"Are you questioning my taste?"

"Of course, not. It's just...." The smirk on Mitch's face told me that I was about to get in trouble, so I stopped short. "Tell me what I'm supposed to like at the concert, and we'll see if I can trust you to DJ for me."

"Whoa! That's more control than he's ever given me." Eddie looked shocked, and I worried I might suddenly be in trouble with him.

Mom's personal ringtone sounded and I was saved. "I gotta take this. Shouldn't be a minute. Probably need to pick up something on the way home." I answered, "What's up, Mom?"

"Hey, Theo. Just wanted to see when you were going to be home."

Something was off. I told Mom and Dad yesterday what I had planned today and they'd said nothing when I'd left this morning.

"I'm headed to get some food and catch a concert. Should be home around four. Was planning on dinner with you guys before I headed to Eddie's." She sighed, which was another strange thing. "You okay?"

Eddie shot me a concerned look.

"Yeah. No need to rush home. But we'll need some time to talk before you go out."

Cryptic wasn't usually her style. She must not like what we needed to discuss.

"Okay. I'll shoot you a text when I'm on my way."

"Thanks. And don't worry. Go have a good time."

"Okay. See you when I get back. Bye." I looked at Eddie and shrugged as I disconnected the call. "I've got no idea what that was about, but I'll find out later. Now let's go before Mitch and I starve to death."

THREE

THE AFTERNOON WAS GREAT. Iris introduced me to some good music. Eddie coaxed me to dance a little and convinced me it didn't matter if I looked like I was flailing about. We stayed for the few hours we planned and then made our way back to the cars and my bike. I tossed the bike into Eddie's Jeep, and he drove me home.

Mom's call made even less sense when I arrived and saw her and Dad. They were on the back deck, and Dad had the grill fired up. Because of our schedules, it'd been more than a year since we'd grilled.

"Hey," I said as I opened the screen door to step outside. They sat at the table, engrossed in their tablets. With the light breeze and shade from the trees, it was very nice. "So what's the big news?"

They both looked at me, then Mom set her tablet aside. "I'm sorry about that," she said. "I shouldn't have called. I hope you didn't worry too much."

"Nah, there were plenty of distractions."

She smiled.

"I hope you're hungry." Dad got up and headed for the

house. He stopped and looked back just as he got to the screen door. "I made the hamburgers you like, and we've got your favorite ice cream for dessert."

It felt like when they had to tell me my guinea pig had died while I was at school. They prepared all my favorite things for dinner that night—with enough food that we could've fed a family four times as big as ours.

Should I press to get information before dinner or wait it out?

"Why don't you get cleaned up while your Dad gets the burgers on. Then we'll talk." Mom picked up her tablet and looked at me. The message was clear—we'll tell you when we're ready.

So that's how they wanted to play. Had I been dropped into a parallel universe? My parents didn't usually act like this, especially now that I was older. I trusted that there was some reason for it.

"Sure." I sounded as upbeat and unsuspicious as possible. "Give me fifteen minutes or so."

She nodded and went back to her reading. I went inside as Dad approached with a tray loaded down with hamburgers—too many of them. He smiled and went out without a word.

I've seen movies where aliens take over people's bodies. I never thought I'd see that here given how unusual we were already. I'd play along and see what bomb dropped over dinner. For secret agents, they weren't doing a very good job of acting like everything was normal.

I stayed upstairs a little longer than I'd planned. I took a long shower and looked at my TOS email. After about twenty minutes, I returned to the deck as Dad took burgers and buns off the grill.

"We were just about to call you down." He put the

platter of food on the table and took a step back looking proud of the spread. Baked beans, fixins, and a fruit and Jell-O salad were on the table too.

"Oh, there you are." Mom carried a bowl of potato salad, another of my favorite things. "I think that's all the food." She looked around the table, set with everything else that we could possibly need. "Let's dig in."

I may have eaten at the concert, but that didn't stop me. My plate nearly overflowed with two burgers, and hearty helpings of the sides.

Once everyone had served themselves and I'd sampled some of the very delicious food, I decided it was time to find out whatever it was. "So are we moving? Is someone visiting we don't want to see? I'm guessing if someone had died, you would've told me by now. So just rip off the Band-Aid and tell me."

They looked at each other, and Dad sighed. "I knew we were making too much out of this."

I chuckled. "If this is how you keep secrets in the field, you might want to go back for some remedial training. Just tell me. I can't imagine—"

"We need you to come to New York with us for a few days. Maybe a week." Dad interrupted, and my mouth dropped open in surprise. "We'll keep it as short as possible."

"What?" I was louder than I meant to, but it summed up how I felt. New York was not in my plans. "You know I have the weeks before school all planned out."

"We know." Mom spoke softly. "We wouldn't take you away if it wasn't important."

This wasn't an ask. Very unusual. There had to be a good reason. I couldn't remember the last time they'd forced me to do anything.

I sighed and ate a mouthful of burger. I didn't know what to do. Part of me wanted to act like a child—get up from the table and storm off to my room. That wasn't really who I was, though. They expected me to be the responsible teenager and TOS agent who would do what was necessary when asked. But this wasn't a mission, and they weren't my bosses. Yes, they were my parents. But it wasn't cool to just assume that my plans could be rearranged.

"I know this isn't exactly fair, Theo, and I can see you don't like it. Here's the situation." Dad rubbed his hand across his forehead and looked at Mom before he continued. "I was contacted today by a good friend from college. We haven't seen each other in about a decade, but we stay in touch. Over the years, he's become quite the music mogul. You might have heard of Glenwood Music. Oliver Glenwood is the CEO, and his daughter is one of the label's biggest stars. Yesterday in Central Park, Oliver and Sofia were nearly abducted at a photo shoot. Their own security just barely prevented it."

So far this seemed more like a job for the police. When I didn't speak up, he continued.

"Because of our covers, Oliver thinks I'm with Homeland and your mom is FBI. He's scared for his family, and because his own highly trained security force can't seem to ensure their safety, he's asked for help. Primarily he wants us to bolster his security. But we'll also see if we can find out who's behind this."

So it *was* a mission. Just not a TOS mission.

"How does this involve me? This isn't my specialty. Couldn't I just stay here and, you know, hang out with John?"

"We think it would be good," Mom said, taking over, "if you came along. The cover would be a family vacation to see an old friend. Plus it'd be easier for you to keep an eye on Sofia since you're the same age."

I'd never heard of Glenwood Music, and I didn't know a singer named Sofia. I should probably ask Eddie or Iris to tell me about her.

But I had TOS work, and I had a research project in progress for my MIT advisor. Not to mention I'd carved out a good bit of time to spend with Eddie.

"Plus, you've never been to New York." Mom tried to sound enthusiastic.

"Why not just tell me what's up?"

"You made such a big deal out of the summer plans you had and your junior year wasn't exactly normal. If we played the parental card and didn't leave you a choice, we thought it'd be easier to accept."

It sucked that they felt like they simply couldn't ask for my help. Maybe I wasn't a great son after all. We ate in silence for a while as I thought. After I'd finished off the burgers I spoke again.

"When do we leave?"

Dad smiled. "I'd like to go in the morning if we can. They've got an event tomorrow night, and Sofia has a concert on Monday evening. It'd be ideal if we could attend both."

I tried to make sure my face didn't betray my thoughts. Eddie wasn't going to take this well. "I'll get packed once I'm back from Eddie's. Anything in particular I need to bring?"

"Bring the usual stuff you like to travel with. We may want to be on comms to make things simpler."

Did Dad clear this with TOS? The use of comms outside an official mission was a no-no.

"And no. TOS doesn't know about this. They don't

need to. As a senior agent, I'll authorize the use of whatever equipment we need and take responsibility for it."

"Mind reader."

We smirked at each other, and he shrugged.

"Thanks, Theo, I appreciate this." Dad looked pleased —but not in a jerk sort of way. "Now we better eat up so this food doesn't go to waste."

FOUR

"Is it over?" My face was buried against Eddie's side. The screaming had stopped, but the scary music continued.

When Eddie flinched instead of answering, I knew it was a good thing that I'd stayed down. The end credit music started a few seconds later, and that's when it felt safe to peek.

"Why did I let you talk me into this show?"

"Because everyone's watched it except us." Eddie looked down to where I was still pressed into his side. The top of my head was nestled in his armpit and the side of my face was against his chest. The longer we'd watched, the more I had sunk down to make it easier to hide from the screen. "I've never seen you freak out like this. We've watched some pretty crazy-town horror flicks, and we usually laugh at them—together."

I didn't know why *Stranger Things* pushed all my buttons, but three episodes into our binge, I wasn't sure I could go on.

"You jumped." I looked up and tried to convince him that my fear wasn't silly.

"I did." The mischievous sparkle in his eyes gave me goose bumps. He could be so damned sexy sometimes. "You, on the other hand, buried yourself."

I grabbed the remote and clicked stop before the next episode could begin. I pushed myself up and swung my leg over, so I straddled him. We wore only shorts—me in cargoes and him in basketball shorts. He had the air-conditioning vent closed, and it was warm enough to justify being shirtless in case his parents came in. Since they were home, the door was ajar, and we were being good.

"Don't mock your boyfriend." I pinned his arms to the bed as I grinned at him, resisting the urge to bite one of his small, dark nipples.

"Just spreading truth. If there'd been space, I think you would've burrowed down so you could get between me and the mattress. Did you think you were gonna get sucked into the TV like in *Poltergeist*?"

"See. There's the mocking again." I released his arms and tickled his sides. He bucked like a rodeo bull released from the chute. Laughter filled the room as he tried to grab my hands, but I was too fast.

He changed tactics and used his hips and legs to force me off him. I ended up on my side while he scrambled to hold me down. I looked sideways at him as he eyed me with a suspicious grin. I allowed him to roll me onto my back, and he did as expected—straddled me like I'd done to him.

It was hot.

The hardness in his shorts made my dick bounce. I wished for his parents to leave the house. But, sadly, there was no tech—or mental abilities—available to make that happen.

The shift in eyes from lust to tenderness sent shockwaves

through me. This wasn't "I need to be naked and sweaty" energy. This vibe had been growning the past few weeks—going back to the end of the school year. We'd been saying *I love you* for a while, but there was more now. The flutters I got from him happened more frequently and with more intensity. The looks, like the one he'd just leveled at me, went straight to my heart. It was perfect, even as it sometimes overwhelmed me.

He leaned in, locked lips on mine and kissed urgently. We were experts at keeping moans in check, but the way his breathing flared meant he was on the edge of getting louder. Slowly, we moved into our favorite make-out position—side by side.

"We've gotta stop," Eddie said between kisses, even though he made no other move to end the moment. "Or there's gonna be a mess."

We tried not to grind on each other, but it was difficult. Sometimes the maneuvering for kisses, knocked our boners together. It didn't matter that I had shorts and underwear on, the sensations were powerful. I found out long ago he was more sensitive than me, and I knew how to play that to my advantage.

"Now who can't handle something?" I raised a questioning eyebrow at him when he shuddered.

Before I could react, he sat up, grabbed one of the pillows, and knocked me in the face.

I got the pillow next to me and hit him in the side of the head. "Two can play this."

"But I've got the advantage from up here." He hit me again and made a grab for my weapon.

We laughed even as he hit me again.

"You think?" I scrambled to my knees. Despite the onslaught, and while I still didn't match his height I went after his torso. Eventually I knocked him down, flat against the mattress.

"No fair. Two minutes for cross-checking."

Just like that the fight was over because we laughed too hard. I crashed down next to him. Between us, I found his hand and locked our fingers together.

Once we calmed down, it was time to say what I didn't want to. "So, I've got to go out of town again."

"You just got back."

At least he didn't sound pissed, which might've been better than the disappointment.

"I know. Not work this time, though. Family thing. We're going to see some college friend of Dad's."

"How'd you get roped into that? You're here all the time when they travel."

"I know." I released his hand, rolled over to my side and propped my head up on my fist. "They pulled the parent card on me."

"Damn." He sounded as surprised as I'd felt earlier. "I didn't think they ever did that to you."

"They usually don't. This means a lot to them, though."

"Do you at least get to go someplace cool?"

"New York. I've never been, so that's something. You might know who we're seeing. Some music guy —Glenwood."

"Are you for real?" Eddie bounded from the bed and went to his desk where he opened his laptop. "That dude's only done some of the best music, like, ever—going back to when he was our age, like, twenty-five years ago."

I hadn't expected he'd shift to excited, or that we'd be back on my lack of music knowledge.

"Didn't I get grief just a few hours ago for listening to old music?"

He looked at me with a mix of shock and disbelief. "There's old and then there's classic. Just listen."

He played a few different songs—some of which I recognized from Dad's collection. Instrumentally they were great, and his voice was pretty good too. I stood behind him to see the song list, so I could grab them from Dad.

It wasn't that I was anti-music. I was just picky. It needed to have some complexity in the rhythm or the vocalist needed to be outstanding. Of course, a perfect blend of instruments and vocals was a ticket to my heart.

"Okay, those were really good," I admitted.

"He's an amazing songwriter and producer. And even though he's got the huge company, he's still creative, working with a lot of his artists. It would be nice if his daughter got all of his talent, but she's mostly just a cookie-cutter teen pop singer. I mean she's great to listen to, but you wouldn't like it."

Eddie brought up YouTube and typed in *Sofia Glenwood*. He played the first video that came up. She was beautiful, black hair pulled back tight and a body I was sure many straight boys fantasized about. He was right. I didn't like it. It was bland without much creativity. Sofia's voice was good, but she just wanted you to know why she'd be the best girlfriend.

Eddie caught my frown. "Exactly. How is she even in the same family? She's famously turned down her father's offer to collaborate. Her stuff sells, though, likely because her voice is good, and she had the family name to work with."

"How do you know all this stuff?"

Eddie shrugged. "I watch TMZ."

I reached around Eddie and did a search to see more about the family. They were gorgeous, and it was surprising that only Sofia was usually in front of a camera. Oliver Glenwood reminded me of Ben Affleck with the chiseled jaw and the perpetual five o'clock shadow. Marcella might as well have been an older Selena Gomez. Sofia was the perfect blending of her parents. Apparently Marcella didn't do too much with the company, instead using her law degree to run the family's foundation, which worked with a number of charities that benefited children, education and equal rights.

"You're gonna have a week with the beautiful people. I think I'm kinda jealous."

"I'm sure." Sarcasm spilled out. "I can't imagine I'll hang around while Mom and Dad catch up with their friends. Besides, I've got work and school stuff to do. I wish you'd be there to explore the city with me. That'd be much better."

"Totally." Eddie spun around in his chair and grabbed my hips before he looked up at me. "Just watch out for Sofia. She's got a rep, and you're a hot guy." He didn't sound like he was kidding either.

"And I'm gay with a boyfriend, so it'd be a waste of her time." I buried my face down in his Afro until I could plant a kiss on his scalp.

He looked up at me. "When will you be back so we can get our summer going again?"

"It shouldn't be more than a week." I stole a look at the clock on the computer screen and saw it was nearly eleven. "I should go. We're headed out early, and I have to pack."

It took several minutes for me to get out of Eddie's room and still more to ride away from his house. This needed to be a short trip because I had a boyfriend to get back to.

FIVE

THE GLENWOODS LIVED IN BROOKLYN. We'd only been off the highway for a few minutes before I wanted to get hold of a bike and ride. Many of the streets reminded me of Boston, but the scenery was different—and changed faster. In the span of just a few blocks we passed short four- and five-story buildings; then there were tall residential towers, and in the middle of it all—Barclays Center. Even though it had a reputation as a crappy place to see a game, I wished it was hockey season.

The major place I wanted to ride was the large park, which our driver said was Prospect Park. It stretched out in the distance as we approached the Glenwood's house. We turned onto a street filled with brownstones and came to a stop midway down the block. I'd expected to stay in Manhattan, not Brooklyn. The idea of a media mogul living in a regular neighborhood like this, even though the building and surroundings were nice, went against everything TV had taught me.

As we got out of the SUV, the front door opened and a good-looking older man came down the stairs, smiling.

Oliver Glenwood was more handsome in person than he'd been on Eddie's computer screen. Even at a distance, he had a certain, confident swagger.

"Victor!" Oliver met Dad at the front of the SUV. They shook hands, laughed a moment, and pulled each other into a bro-hug. Mom and I stopped at Dad's side.

As Oliver kissed Mom's cheek and hugged her, I noticed the black-suited man at the top of the steps, just outside the front door. Definitely a security guy because I didn't imagine a butler-type looking like he could take someone out.

The street was pretty cool with all the different brown-stones packed closely together. It seemed sad, though, that no one had a front yard. At least there were trees along the sidewalk that kept things nicely shaded.

"This is Theo." Dad saying my name snapped me back from surveying the surroundings.

"Theo, sorry they dragged you up here." Oliver extended his hand to me and I met it—strong grip to strong grip.

"No worries, Mr. Glenwood. I've never been to New York, so it'll be cool to check it out."

"Please, call me Oliver." I nodded.

Another man dodged around the security guy to get out of the house. This one was in a polo shirt and jeans.

"This is my assistant, Christian. These are my friends Victor, Katherine, and their son, Theo."

Christian exuded efficiency as he looked us over and smiled. "Welcome. I'll get the bags."

"So I thought we'd give you the guest suite." Oliver pointed to the building next to the one he'd come out of. "The first floor is a full one-bedroom apartment, so you'll have some privacy. Theo, figuring you don't want to stay on a couch, you can take the studio below it."

Score! My own place for however long we were here. A definite perk.

"Cool. Thanks."

"Hopefully it makes the visit more comfortable."

Christian took things out of the back of the SUV, but I went to grab my backpack before he could take it. "I'll get that, thanks." I wasn't keen on my stuff in someone else's hands. Thankfully no one questioned it.

"Come on in and I'll show you around... and we can talk."

We followed Oliver. As we approached the front door, the security guy stepped inside and waited, out of the way, so we could pass. Once I was in, he resumed his place, leaving the door open. Maybe he kept watch on Christian and the luggage? I didn't stay behind to find out.

"Marcella sends her regrets she couldn't be here for your arrival. She'll be home later." We paused in the entryway and he gestured to his left. "This is the more formal living room. It's really a throwback to the way my parents had it when I was growing up."

The room was well kept but clearly stuck in time. The furniture was functional and stylish in a sixties or seventies sort of way. Upstairs the space was impressive as it opened up to the entire floor.

"This is incredible," Dad said. "I didn't realize you'd joined the buildings together."

"You knew I bought this building when my parents were ready to sell and move to Palm Beach a few years ago." Dad nodded. "When the other building went on the market last year I snapped it up, and we expanded. Third floor has offices for me and Marcella, along with the master suite and the top floor is Sofia's, including a small recording studio. The ground floor of this side is the base for my onsite security team."

Dad's "incredible" was an understatement. I always thought our house, Eddie's house, Mitch's house were nice, comfortable. This amped all that up, but it didn't seem like too much either. It reflected good taste. The colors were soft, and there was a lot of wood and brick. I wouldn't call it modern, but it wasn't old either.

"Have a seat." Oliver gestured to the dining room, where there was a large wood table surrounded with ten chairs. Like the rest of the furnishings, it was beautiful— probably reclaimed wood from the looks of it. "Let me get lunch."

He gets the lunch? For someone whose daughter lived her life on TMZ, or so Eddie made me think, he was very down to earth. He could be one of our neighbors. If I didn't already know what he did, I'd have no clue he owned a hugely successful company. The entire space invited you to get comfortable.

"I can get that, Oliver." Christian hit the top of the stairs and headed for the kitchen, which was defined by a large breakfast bar. I loved that you could see from the windows along the back wall of the kitchen on through to the huge windows that looked out from the living room. There were no visible blinds so perhaps no privacy on this level.

Oliver returned to the table and sat next to me. I wondered if he had the need to balance the table with my parents on the other side.

"So tell us what's happened." Dad straightened in his chair and shifted into his authoritative all-business voice.

Oliver nodded. "Two days ago Sofia and I were in Central Park for a photo shoot for her next album. It attracted a fair amount of attention because word spread on social media that we were there. Three guys rushed us from nowhere. Thankfully we were able to manage it, but they almost had Sofia in an SUV before my guys got their act together." Panic flashed in his eyes. "We were in the northern part of the park and regular vehicles aren't allowed up there, so how did they even get in? And why can no one figure out who they are? It's like they disappeared."

Christian brought a platter of sandwiches and set it down. After another trip to the kitchen, he returned with a bowl of green salad. Oliver followed Christian back to retrieve dishes and a pitcher of water.

"Is that the first time anything like this has happened?" Dad asked.

"No," Oliver said as he passed out dishes. I liked the casual, homey vibe. "I haven't told Marcella or Sofia, but last week, coming back from LA, I'm convinced someone masquerading as a TSA agent tried to take me. I went through security at LAX and got pulled aside as I was getting my bags from the X-ray. The agent asked me to follow. I'm Pre and Global Entry, so I'm about as cleared as it gets but I went along with it. We went through a door and walked along a corridor that went on and on. Two other TSA agents approached and asked where he was taking me. He said he'd gotten lost since it was his first week on the job. They guided him back to an interview room and one of them stayed as I was taken through a weird interview about why I was traveling and what was in my luggage."

"But they let you go?" Dad encouraged him to continue.

"Yeah. The agent who'd stayed back reviewed my info and told me it was a clear glitch in the system. She apologized and walked me out. She said she'd speak with the other agent to make sure he understood what to look for in the future. I didn't think any more of it. But after the park incident, it seems like we might be targets."

Oliver filled his plate, and the rest of us followed suit. No one ate, though.

"Has anything unusual been going on?" Mom picked up with the questions. "Recently fired people with a grudge? Business deals that went sideways?"

Oliver shrugged. "No more than usual. My team's vetted the people who have left the company—both fired and leaving on their own—from the past six months. No red flags. As for business deals. We turn things down all the time, but none of it seems out of the ordinary. We can re-review if you think it'd reveal anything."

"Why don't you let us do it?" Dad asked. "If it's someone inside your organization, you might get false information back."

"Won't you raise more suspicions?"

Mom and Dad looked at each other.

"No." Dad smiled, and Oliver seemed to relax. "Just tell us the employees and the companies we need to look at and we'll take it from there. What about your personal security?"

"I'm worried they can't do the job. There were four of them in the park and... well."

"We'll examine security from top to bottom." Mom looked to Dad. "I'll take physical security. We'll use Theo's expertise to examine your IT network and see if there're any red flags there." Her eyes darted to me as she mentioned my name, and I nodded.

Oliver's brow wrinkled as he tried to reconcile that bit of information. "You're a security expert?" It was cool he looked at me as he asked and not my parents. He managed to not sound condescending either, even though he wasn't sure.

"Yes, sir." I reached into my back pocket, pulled my wallet, and fished out a business card. These were for show, but I kept a couple on me just in case. "I have a consulting firm." I handed over the card and he studied it. It was plain white with "Theodore Reese—Cyber Security Specialist" in two lines at the center of the card. In the lower corners were an email address and phone number.

"He's been brilliant with computers for years, and he's taken courses at MIT for the past two years." I didn't get to see Mom be the proud parent very often, so it was nice to see her light up talking about my accomplishments.

"Impressive."

"Thanks." We traded nods.

"So, we've got an event tonight that I'm honestly a little scared to go to," he said. "That's why I hoped you'd come up today to see if you could augment the security detail."

Oliver went over the arrangements. His wife was getting an award from the Ali Forney Center for her work advocating for LGBTQ+ homeless youth through the Glenwood Foundation. The evening's program included a cocktail hour and dinner along with Oliver doing the introduction, he and Sofia performing and then Marcella accepting with a speech. All in all, it should take about three hours. Their security would be at the perimeter of the room but given the event they would keep it low key and not make anyone nervous.

"I've made space at our table for you three. It is black tie, so I've also arranged for our stylists to come and outfit you since I neglected to mention formal wear."

"Good call," Dad said. "Because we don't have that at home either. Do you by chance have a guest list for the event and the vendors working it? We've got time to run checks on them."

"I can get it." He pulled out his phone and typed. "What else do you need?"

Mom and Dad looked at each other, and I took the moment to speak up. "I'd like to get the IPs for your servers." Oliver took a note of that also.

"Do you want to talk to someone in IT?"

"Not necessary. Just the addresses will be enough, so I don't have to search it out. Since I'm looking for vulnerabilities, the less they know for now the better."

He smiled and tapped my card on the tabletop. "All right. What are you looking for?"

"Any signs that you've had a breach. If someone's in there, they may have accessed information that they could use to come after your family."

"You'll let me know what you find?"

"For sure." I smiled back.

"Let us get unpacked." Mom stood and the rest of us followed. "We'll get our investigations started and develop strategy around tonight as well."

"Thank you." Oliver sounded relieved. "I'll get all the information you asked for to you within the hour. Please take some food. I'm sure you must need something after the trip."

Christian appeared from the kitchen area. He must've been listening to know when we'd wrapped up. "I'll take you to your rooms to make sure you get settled. After that I'm happy to deliver some food."

This trip may not be so boring after all.

SIX

HAVING my own apartment was pretty epic. Too bad this was all about work. As I checked out the space, I considered the many ways Eddie and I could play house here.

I unpacked—at least the high-tech stuff. The clothes could stay in the bag, and I'd just fish out whatever when I needed it. Anyone who came in would think I'd just brought a regular laptop and a tablet, and not super secure TOS devices. They operated on my TOS Wi-Fi hotspot. I also made sure they left a footprint on the household Wi-Fi Christian had given us access to. That ensured nothing would appear abnormal if anyone looked at what was connected. Mom and Dad were no doubt upstairs doing the same for the electronics.

I was about to call Eddie to show him this place when a knock interrupted. Through the glass set in the front door, I saw Christian and some other guy who held clothing bags by hangers.

Might as well get this over with. Give me jeans, T-shirts, or sweatshirts and I'm good. I owned a few dressier outfits, which were mostly to wear on game days because Coach made us wear suits. I had one really good suit too. I got it when Eddie and I went to junior prom last year. I had a feeling I wouldn't like anything I'd have to wear tonight, though. Luckily, I only had to be in it for a few hours.

"Hey, Christian, come on in." I opened the door wide to let them enter.

"Theo this is Frederick. He works with Oliver's favorite clothier. He's got some suits for you to try for the event."

While Christian was dressed comfortably, Frederick looked like he'd walked out of *GQ*. I felt underdressed in khaki shorts, polo shirt, and sneakers.

"You gave me a good description," Frederick said to Christian. "I've brought some clothes that will have you looking sharp."

"Great." I tried to sound upbeat about it because I needed to fit in tonight.

There were times I felt like I lived in a movie, especially on missions. This was one of those moments. I'd never had clothes brought to me, and I didn't go to fancy events either. Staying focused on the mission aspect helped keep the anxiety in check.

"I'll leave you to it." Christian headed for the door but turned back before he got there. "Theo, pick wisely. Oliver's arranged for you to keep what you select as a thank you."

"Cool. Thanks." That was nice. I grinned at the idea of having a new prom outfit without having to do any of the shopping.

Christian nodded and zipped out of the apartment leaving me with Frederick.

"Okay. We may have to do some on-the-fly alterations, but I don't think this will take too long. I brought in three suits, but there's more in the van if you don't like them."

"I'm sure what you've got here will be fine."

Frederick, who didn't seem much older than me, looked me over. Scrutinized might be a better word for it. The urge to fidget was tough to beat down. "You've never done anything like this before?"

I chuckled. "No. I bought a suit last year at Macy's and my boyfriend made sure it looked okay."

He nodded. "Try to have a little fun with this then. Pick out what you really like, and I'll make sure it fits perfectly. Are you still growing?"

I don't think anyone other than my grandma had ever asked me that question. I shrugged. "I don't think I've gotten taller in a while."

"Good. We'll leave a touch of room just in case, nothing too obvious. You'll be able to wear this for quite some time."

"For all those times I wear a tuxedo?"

Frederick laughed. It didn't seem like a mean laugh, but it was hard to tell. "I haven't brought true tuxedos. There are no bow ties or cummerbunds. You could wear this anywhere you'd dress up."

"Um. Okay."

"Don't worry. You'll see. Get your clothes off and let's see what looks good on you."

He turned to the bags he'd laid over the couch and unpacked as I toed off my sneakers and stripped. When he turned back, that analytical gaze returned as I stood in my boxers and socks.

"Can I make a purely professional observation?"

"I guess." Might as well hear what he had to say.

"You really should wear more fitted shirts. You're in shape so there's no reason to be oversized all the time."

Heat rose in my cheeks and I fought the urge to cover myself. I usually didn't care who I was naked in front of—although I wasn't totally naked now. I'd done it enough in locker rooms that it didn't matter. And Eddie and I complemented each other a lot. I knew I had a decent body, but no one but Eddie commented about how I looked. I should've expected he'd notice the polo I'd worn was larger than it needed to be. Comfort more than anything dictated the clothes I wore.

"Sorry. It's a hazard of the job to pay so much attention to what a customer wears." He smiled, and it put me at ease. He handed me pants and then laid out a shirt and jacket on the couch back before looking around the small apartment. "No mirror. I'll get the one from the van. Go ahead and put these on."

He dashed out, and I dressed. The pants and jacket were jet black while the shirt was stark white. As Frederick returned, I fiddled with the pants because they were too loose, and no belt was in sight.

"Here, let me get a belt for that." Frederick set the mirror down against the wall across from me. He went to another bag that he'd already brought in. Even though the suit wasn't quite the right size, I could tell that it looked good on me. "Here. You'll be able to see what it looks like without holding your pants up."

I got the belt on and let my arms fall to my side. I felt a little silly. Frederick stood next to me and looked into the mirror. "It's not bad for the first try. Do you think you want to go with basic black or do you want a little bit of color?"

I shrugged.

"I brought a few things. Nothing too flashy. Let's try a few and see what you think. And then we can do any alterations."

It seemed like he had an endless supply of clothes in the van. Over the next half hour, I tried on various combinations of shirts and suits. We finally settled on charcoal for the suit and a shirt that was the lightest of gray. Frederick also talked me into suspenders. I liked how they looked with the jacket off, so I went with them. What neither of us could decide on was the color of the tie. We finally chose a subtle pop of color with a grayish-blue. I'd never looked this good.

"So, what do you think?" Instead of next to me, this time Frederick stood by the mirror and looked me over.

I studied myself, hands in my pockets, jacket unbuttoned. "I don't really know what to say." It was lame, but true. I didn't usually boast about clothes or my appearance. "It does look pretty good."

"You don't have to be so modest. You're allowed to compliment yourself."

"I wish my boyfriend was here to see it. He'd love it."

"We can snap a couple pictures, so you can show him."

Going through poses at Frederick's direction as he snapped pictures for Eddie felt totally silly but fun. He had photography skills, and the pics were some of the best I'd taken.

"Thanks." I flipped through the pictures a couple of times trying to decide what to send Eddie, and ultimately I sent all five. He might as well have the entire fashion spread since it was unlikely this would ever happen again.

"Okay. I think you're good to go. I'm going to leave you a few options for the tie and pocket square just in case you want to mix up the colors. These will all look good with your complexion and the suit. On the house."

"Are you sure? The one is totally fine."

Frederick gathered up what we didn't use. "For sure. You were fun to work with, and I could tell you had a hard time making up your mind about the color. No one will notice if I come back with fewer accessories."

My phone chirped with Eddie's text tone. "Let's see what Eddie thought of what we put together." I opened his text.

Whoa! Look at you. What are you doing down there? You look hot. And I'm jealous I'm not there to see it in person.

"He approves," I told Frederick.

I replied: *Don't worry. You'll be able to see it when I get back. I get to keep it, so I'll do a fashion show for you.*

He responded quickly: *You need to hurry up and come back, then, because I'm going to end up drooling on these pictures waiting for you.*

"Good," Frederick said. "If he didn't, I'd worry that he didn't have good taste."

He smiled, and I chuckled. "Believe me, he's got much more style sense than I do. Do you need any help getting everything to the van?"

"You don't have to do that," he said as he packed his things. "You're the client, after all."

I changed back into my normal clothes because I didn't want to get the suit messed up. "Actually, I think Oliver's the client and I'm just a lucky recipient. Let me help you out."

It only took a few minutes for us to get all the stuff in the van. He didn't go immediately, however, his coworkers were still working with my parents. I was going to go up with him, but my phone vibrated. It was Lorenzo on a secure line, so I had to take it.

Once in the apartment, I connected the call.

"Winger, Dr. Possible here." He used the usual greeting.

"Hey, Doc, what can I do for you?"

"I wanted to see if your location was secure enough that

I can courier you the new prototype of the lenses. I wanted to get you the latest so you could test."

Awesome! I'd been eager for these and finally, after a couple of weeks, they were ready. It looked like this would be the last test run.

"I'm secure enough if the courier can put them directly into my hands." I gave him the address and let him know which door was mine.

"I'll have them contact you when they're a few minutes away to make sure you can accept. Use them as much as you can to put them through their paces. Hemingway, Walker, and I will do the same."

The lenses might help on this pseudo assignment too. We'd be able to get images without being obvious. "I'll make sure to thoroughly test them."

"How's New York?" Lorenzo asked, shifting topics. "I was surprised when you said you were going."

"Fine, I guess. Only been here a few hours so far. Met Defender's friend and that was cool. We're staying in a spiffy brownstone in Brooklyn, and I've got my own apartment."

"Your own space. Nice! I remember plenty of trips with my parents where we were all crammed up in a hotel room, so you've got it made." We traded a few family travel stories before we got back around to the package delivery.

"I'll let you know when I have them and keep you posted on testing."

"Sounds good. Talk later." Lorenzo disconnected the call.

I hadn't expected the contact lenses. We'd designed them to be used in the field for night vision, heat vision, transmitting video, and more. I'd worked on and off over the past six months on the app that paired with the lenses.

Perfected, they would revolutionize gathering intel and the environments agents could work in.

I had about five hours before the reception. Now that I was on my own, I could pull up information about tonight's event space. The more we knew going in, the more we'd be able to plan for the unexpected.

My phone buzzed with a text. It was Mom. She wanted me to come upstairs once I saw the van with the stylists leave. They wanted to get our plan together. Hopefully nothing would happen since this was a charity event, but given the brazen attempt in Central Park, we needed to be on our toes tonight.

SEVEN

I'D NEVER BEEN to anything like this. Five hundred people stuffed into a ballroom at a fancy hotel near Union Square. Luckily I didn't mind crowds because, despite trying to stay on the periphery to watch people, I kept getting drawn into conversations. The event proved to be an excellent test for the contact lenses because I tried to look at everyone, so we could run checks on who was here.

A number of people my age were in attendance—some used the Ali Forney Center's programs while others were volunteers. I was a little embarrassed at my good fortune as I heard stories from these teenagers. I wasn't naïve. Sometimes kids were bounced out of their home for coming out. I couldn't imagine not having a home, not to mention figuring out shelter and food every day. I would definitely donate to this organization and find out if there was something similar in Boston.

The reception before dinner was easygoing—people milled around talking, having appetizers and drinks, and looking at items in a silent auction. The forty-five minutes passed quickly.

Oliver Glenwood stayed close to my dad while Marcella was near Mom. I had yet to meet Sofia. Apparently she was coming straight from the recording studio. Christian assured Oliver that she'd be on time for at least dinner so that her arrival wouldn't be a distraction.

As the charity's director came to the podium to give brief remarks, the daughter of the honoree had still not arrived. Dinner was to come right after these remarks. In the research I'd done, the press presented Sofia as someone with a rebellious streak. However, she did seem to stay close to her family and attend functions with them. Maybe her delay was as simple as traffic. With the issues that had occurred, however, the fact that no one seemed to know her exact location bothered me.

As the speech continued, I moved closer to where my parents stood with the Glenwoods near the front of the crowd. I silently came up next to Dad who must've caught me out of the corner of his eye. He gave me a smile and put his arm around my shoulders for a brief hug. The speech, which talked about the number of kids who were on the street because they'd come out, no doubt pulled on his parental heartstrings.

When the speech concluded, the attendees were directed to the dining room. As the crowd filed out, Sofia quietly slipped through a side door and came up to her parents.

She wasn't what I expected. The entourage and flashier clothes were missing. She was dressed as elegantly as the rest of us and looked as poised as Marcella.

The six of us stayed together near the rear of the crowd.

"Sofia." Oliver sounded very happy to see her. "Glad you're here."

"Yes, I was beginning to think I'd be left with an empty

chair next to me." Her mother, speaking with a slight accent, leaned in and gave her a quick kiss on the cheek.

"I'd never do that to you. At least not without calling first." Sofia flashed a huge smile and returned Marcella's kiss. "Plus, you know I've got a song for you."

"Sofia I'd like you to meet the Reeses," Oliver said. "This is Victor." He gestured at my dad. "He's the college friend I told you about who works for Homeland." Oliver spoke in hushed tones. "This is Katherine, an agent with the FBI, and their son, Theo, who, it turns out, is a cybersecurity expert."

Sofia nodded but didn't step away from her parents to shake hands or offer any other greeting. "Man, you must have a helluva time getting away with stuff. I thought I had it tough with security on me all the time."

"You have no idea." She and I laughed. It was the right small talk to make with her, even though I never tried to get away with anything.

"Sofia, over the next few days the Reeses will be with us as much as our security is. They're going to help us figure out what's going on. Theo's going to be hanging with you as part of that."

Sofia looked like she was hearing this for the first time and was none too pleased about it. In fact I'm sure I had the same expression when I heard I was coming to New York.

"Can we talk about this later? I don't see how this dude's gonna fit in with my crowd and I don't see what the point is if he obvs doesn't belong. No offense, man."

"None taken. I'm sure we can work something out. But you're right. This isn't the place to talk."

"We'll save this for home." Oliver made it clear the topic was closed. "We should head to dinner. We don't want to keep the honoree from some hotel chicken." He smiled proudly at his wife.

The room had emptied out of everyone but us and two of Oliver's guards.

Oliver took Marcella's hand, and they walked out as Dad and Mom followed closely at their side. I drifted slightly behind so they could get through the doorway and was surprised that Sofia fell in step next to me.

"Seriously, man," Sofia said quietly, "I'm sure you're a nice guy and probably good at what you do, but there's no way my friends'll believe we'd be hanging out."

"I get it. I have no problem feeling awkward if it keeps you safe. I'm sure we can come up with a story for why I'm suddenly staying close."

Sofia shrugged. I hadn't noticed when she arrived, but she walked with just a little bit of strut. Was it arrogance? Confidence? Fake? I couldn't read it. Was it more pronounced when she wasn't at an event like this or when she was around the posse she was trying to keep me out of? I guessed I'd figure it out over the next few days.

In the dining room, we made our way to the front because the family needed to be near the stage. Oliver and Sofia had their presentations, and Marcella would speak. All of that would happen after dinner.

The five men of Oliver's security team were easy to spot. One of the things Mom or Dad needed to do was train these men to blend in better because it would make it more difficult for anyone trying to make trouble because they couldn't tell who was on guard.

We were at a circular table that sat eight. And the Glenwood's were surrounded by us. Mom was next to Marcella with Oliver next to his wife. Dad was flanked by him and

Sofia while I was on the other side of her. The director of the organization and her wife rounded out the table.

The ballroom was loud as everyone chattered throughout dinner. The conversation at our table remained educational, at least for me and probably for my parents too, as we found out more about the organization Marcella devoted so much time to.

"So you're seriously some major computer expert?" Sofia asked during a lull in the table conversation. "I mean I know guys who design video games and do music and whatever but security?"

"I've had a knack for computers for as long as I can remember, and I went into security because I really enjoy the problem solving and the algorithms. And as long as I'm good at it, I might as well earn some money too."

"Cool that people pay you. Do you work for anyone I might know?"

I shrugged. "Afraid I can't tell you. Everything I do is under non-disclosures because no one wants their security info made public."

"I hear that." I had Sofia's undivided attention. I thought she'd sit at dinner and be bored with the conversation since it didn't exactly fit the lifestyle the media portrayed for her. Even when it was our parents talking, she still seemed engaged. "It's hard to keep the music under wraps these days. Everybody wants to get the early track. It's ridiculous. I know Dad has a huge cyber team to keep all the music secure. Not just preventing leaks but also trying to keep the streaming channels and digital stores secure."

The problem stretched across all the entertainment industries. There were stories about companies like HBO targeted by hackers who leaked programs early. And piracy of movies, music, and books had been a problem for as long as the internet had been around.

"Can you do work like that?" Sofia asked.

"The principals of what I do would apply for sure. If your dad wants, maybe I can look over what his team's already doing."

"Since we're going to spend time together, maybe you can give me some tips on how to keep my stuff as secure as possible between my home setup, the studio, and when it gets released."

"Sure. I bet we can make time for that."

"Cool, man." Sofia put out her fist, and I bumped it.

Oliver leaned over and kissed Marcella on the cheek before he got up. It must be time for the program to start. Oliver made his way to the stage and took note cards out of his jacket pocket as he walked.

The lights lowered, although not down to completely dark. The stage was brightly lit, with an extra bright spot on the podium. Oliver had everyone's attention even before he stepped to the mic.

"I want to thank you all for coming tonight and donating some of your hard-earned cash to help support the Ali Forney Center and its efforts to eradicate homelessness among LGBTQ youth in New York City. In particular I'm honored to pay tribute to my wife, Marcella, who works tirelessly with this organization to help accomplish its mission."

I took a moment to scan the crowd. With everyone seated, it would be even easier to record with the lenses. No one looked out of place among those I could easily see without being too awkward.

Oliver spoke for several minutes, interrupted more than once by applause. Marcella sometimes dabbed at her eyes with a tissue she'd pulled from her handbag.

"I'd like to ask our daughter, Sofia, to join me." As Oliver spoke, three men brought out a keyboard along with two more microphones. "This collaboration marks a first for us, and it seemed appropriate to join forces to honor Marcella." Sofia got up, kissed her mom and hugged her shoulders before going to the stage. "We've written—and, yes, you heard that right—*we've* written a special song. Marcella, this is for you."

Father and daughter hugged before Oliver stepped behind the keyboard, and Sofia came out front to the microphone.

"Before we start, Mom, I want you to know how proud I am that you do what you do. Not everyone is as lucky as I am to have such wonderful parents. 'Guardian' is for you, Mom."

I'd only heard a couple of Sofia's songs last night before I left Eddie's. This had a distinctly different, more complex melody. Even before Sofia sang a single note, I liked it. Then Sofia started, her voice wrapped around the music in a gorgeous marriage. The lyrics spoke of a strong woman who defended those who could not protect themselves.

The similarities between Sofia and Oliver as they performed were striking. They were lost in the music, but they also occasionally looked directly at Marcella as if she was the only one in the room. Out of the corner of my eye, I saw her get a second tissue.

This was a song I'd download because it had a great rhythm, meaningful lyrics, and soaring vocals. Hearing her live made me wonder if she used electronics on her voice because she didn't sound like this on her recordings.

As Oliver played the final chords, Sofia bowed and blew a kiss to her mom.

The audience got to their feet, cheering. Oliver came

forward and put his arm around Sofia's shoulders, and they both bowed.

Oliver stepped close to the mic and held up his hand to get the audience's attention. "We'll release that song tomorrow for purchase. All proceeds will go directly to AFC to continue to help those who need it the most." The audience cheered louder. "All of you here tonight can get an early copy. We have them available for purchase at a special price that will also get you an autograph from Sofia and myself. Those are available at the tables in the back. Thank you for your support."

The lights went out.

For a moment it seemed like a glitch—the wrong button pushed to bring up the lighting on the audience perhaps. When it continued more than a couple seconds the hairs on the back of my neck stood up.

I blinked four times rapidly to bring up the contact lenses' menu. I activated the night vision.

Everything went green and it took me a minute to adjust because I wasn't used to working in this mode. Four men moved confidently and quickly around the tables, and they had night-vision goggles on. Oliver's security blindly felt their way along the walls, trying to get to the stage.

While the lenses were supposed to be a secret, even from my parents, I had to say something because Dad was getting up and had no idea what the threats were.

"Dad!" I yelled to be heard over the crowd who talked louder the longer the lights were out. "Four men with night vision. Mom, keep hold of Marcella. Dad," I said as I got up, "I'm coming around for you and we're going to the stage."

"Theo, can you see my purse?" Mom asked. "Can you put it in my hand."

I loved my family--no one even asked why I could see.

"Yeah. Right here." As I passed her, on my way to Dad, I put her hand on it.

I grabbed Dad's shoulder and told him to stay close. "Sofia and Oliver haven't moved."

"New gadget, huh?" Dad asked quietly.

"Yeah. Glad I decided to use this as a field test." I looked behind us. "The four guys are spreading out. I don't see guns, but I assume they're armed."

We got to the stage, and I guided us to step up.

"It's Theo and Victor." It was weird using Dad's first name. "We're right here. Katherine's got Marcella."

I reached out and grabbed Sofia just below the elbow. Then I guided Dad's hand to Oliver's arm.

"What's happening?" Oliver sounded panicked, a surprise given how calm he'd been so far in discussing the past abduction attempts.

"Four men in the room," Dad said. "They've got goggles. Theo?"

"They're having a hard time getting up here. People keep getting in their way. Having the tables so close together is making it difficult, especially as panic grows."

"We should get you out of here," Dad said. "Theo, I can keep these two. Can you get your mom and Marcella out?"

Light illuminated our table. It looked like Mom activated her flashlight app. The night vision blotted out in that area leaving me with just a peripheral. It would do the same for the bad guys.

More phones lit up, making it increasingly hard for me to see. I blinked and brought up the menu for the lenses and chose to keep one eye on night vision and one normal.

"Mom's got Marcella safe," I said. "Let's get these two into a more secure area."

Oliver's security had one of the guys. Another was

about to be apprehended as he struggled to get his goggles off. Mom indicated an exit just off the stage to our left. Dad and I nodded in acknowledgment.

Despite the phone lighting, people scrambled to get to the exits causing general chaos. I'd lost track of the other two guys. With the night vision activated I wasn't able to accurately see details, so I didn't have any idea what they looked like. If they ditched their goggles they could blend in.

We moved to the exit door staying close together. Marcella and Mom were going there too when they were tackled to the floor by a woman in a ball gown.

That wasn't an accident—the woman was not someone trying to get away.

Oliver broke away from Dad and went to help.

"Get her out of here," Dad called to me as he went after Oliver.

My grip on Sofia's arm tightened. "Come on."

"No way, man. I'm not leaving my family."

I moved us toward the exit despite her resistance. I leaned into her—not as forcefully as I would a defenseman but enough to get us moving. "No. We're leaving here now."

She jerked against my hold but couldn't break it.

"Let me go!" She was furious.

"My parents got this." I pulled her with me. "We're going out that door."

The scene couldn't be easy for her to witness. I didn't like it either. Mom grappled with the woman who'd attacked them. Dad had Oliver and Marcella on a path for the rear doors of the dining room. Dad's mouth moved but I couldn't hear him over the noise. We should've been on comms. My earpiece was in, but only to record audio for the lenses.

There were no guns in sight. The team must only be interested in getting their hands on the family without injuries. Sofia and I got to the door. According to the plans I'd studied earlier it would lead into a service corridor and ultimately to the kitchen. From there we'd be able to get into a stairwell that would exit onto the street.

The door pushed open easily and we slipped through. It was pitch black. Did they cut the electricity to the entire building? It would've been easy enough to control the lighting in the dining room, but it seemed extreme to take out more than that.

"We need to go back." Sofia jerked hard against my hold. I stopped us a few steps inside the corridor. "We can't even see in here."

"I can." I adjusted the lenses so both eyes could see. "We have to go. Our parents are expecting us to get outside."

The door burst open behind us. I turned and found a man pulling goggles over his eyes. I swung Sofia around behind me.

"Hey!" Sofia shouted in surprise.

I got into a defensive stance as the guy charged me.

"I only want the girl," the attacker said. "Don't make me go through you."

My heart raced as the adrenaline pumped. It was time to trust my training.

"Sofia, get outta here. Run for it!"

"Why are you making this difficult?" The man sounded exasperated. The corridor was wide enough that three or four people could walk side by side. He tried to go around, but I dodged in front of him, continually making myself an obstacle. He apparently didn't want to engage in a fight.

"I can't see, man. How am I supposed to run?" Sofia whined, her tough facade faltering.

"It's a straight line down the hall." I kept focus on blocking the guy as I shouted instructions. "Keep your hand against the wall and go."

The guy finally had enough of the dodge and weave. He tried to grab me, but I got his arm instead. I crouched down to lower my center of gravity and pulled him hard toward me. He cried out. Was it surprise or pain?

The click of Sofia's heels told me she was on the move.

I punched the guy, ensuring I knocked his goggles askew. He was dazed and ended up losing his goggles altogether. To ensure he stayed in the dark, I crushed the lenses under my shoe. I debated incapacitating him more but decided to take off after Sofia instead.

"The kids are headed for the kitchen." His voice was slightly slurred.

Great. They've got comms.

I turned back and hit him in the side of the head with my open hand—a move I learned from John. He staggered into the wall before crumpling to the floor. I couldn't have him reporting anything else. Sofia was down the hall, and I sprinted to get to her.

EIGHT

In a few seconds, I caught up to Sofia. She moved slower than I'd care for, but she did what I told her to do. She stopped as I came up behind her.

"Keep moving!" I didn't slow down. I took her by the elbow and forced her to keep pace. "We gotta go. That guy told them we were here."

Some light leaked through the window in the kitchen door but not much. I adjusted again, so I had one eye with normal vision. Through the window I saw people at work apparently trying to store the food. Hopefully it was only hotel staff. Two battery-powered lanterns provided the light.

The staff paid no attention to us as I searched for the exits—one would go to the fire exit staircase while the other would go out into the lobby that serviced the ballrooms. I wanted the exit and since we were on the sixth floor we didn't have too far to go down.

Sofia didn't say anything. I wasn't sure if she was stunned or just letting me lead. As long as she kept moving, I didn't care.

With all the prep tables and racks, it was difficult to get my bearings. "Which way to the exit?" I shouted.

A woman looked up from her task of covering trays of food with foil. "There."

She pointed to a darkened exit sign. How had even the battery backup failed? None of the emergency lighting was on. This was a very elaborate setup.

Sofia tripped over her feet just as we got to the door. "You okay?"

"Not really." I stopped and saw the fear in her eyes. "What the hell is happening? Where are we going?"

She righted herself and I pushed the release bar to open the door to the dark staircase.

"Whatever it is, we're going to get out of here and it'll be okay."

She nodded and took a deep breath. We stepped into the stairwell.

There was no one above, but I could see people on the stairs below us. The nearest person seemed to be a couple of floors down, and the spots of white indicated they carried phones or flashlights. These were most likely guests trying to get out.

"Do you have your phone?" I pulled mine out and navigated to the flashlight app.

"No." She sighed, and I felt her tremble under my hand. "It's at the table."

I deactivated night vision as I turned on the light.

"We'll be okay," I said with total confidence. "You should take off those shoes. Those heels can't be easy when we're trying to move fast."

She thought about that for a moment and ultimately slipped them off.

I shined the flashlight on the stairs. Sofia followed

without me keeping a hand on her. She kept up with my pace, which wasn't quite a run but was on the faster side. I stopped us short of the third floor as a door burst open. A woman made an unexpected grab at me, and I jumped backward into Sofia, causing her to sit down on the stairs with an "oof."

"I've got 'em. In the third floor, northside stairwell."

She was dressed in a nondescript way—jeans, top, sneakers. She could've been anyone. We moved at the same time. I moved to kick, wanting to knock her into the wall. She stepped back, out of range. She produced a small gun from the waistband.

I froze.

There was no way she'd shoot unless provoked, so I relaxed my stance and put my hands up.

"That's right," she said. "I don't want to hurt anybody."

The door above us clacked open and, based on the loud steps, at least two people were coming down.

"All right, Sofia, get up." The woman gestured with the gun. She pulled me close so Sofia had space to stand.

Sofia grabbed the railing and stood, looking defeated.

The only option was to let this play out. I hated that, but it was the safe way to go.

Two guys came up behind Sofia and one put their hand on her shoulder. The woman in charge of all this grabbed my arm and moved me to the door. The guys shoved Sofia, and she walked ahead of them.

"I'm taking this." She plucked my phone out of my grip. "I'm sure when Oliver figures out she's missing, your phone will be the first one that rings since you two were so chummy tonight."

Besides Oliver knowing we fled together, Mom and Dad could find me easily. They could get in touch with

Lorenzo to track the chip in my neck or the phone. It would give them the upper hand locating us wherever we went. Sofia and I had to stay together.

"Let's get them to the room. We'll hang out there until the power's back, and then we'll take her just like we planned. We'll even take him as a bonus."

"Won't that be risky when everyone can see?" I asked.

"I suspect you two will fit quite nicely in laundry carts that we'll wheel right out." She looked between Sofia and me as she opened the door to her room, which she'd left ajar by swinging out the lock on the inside.

I moved toward the center of the room. I stopped between the two beds so that there was space to maneuver if needed. Sofia stayed close, looking even more terrified.

"Good to see you know when to play nice." The woman looked at me like she was trying to figure out who I was. "Why'd you run with Sofia?"

I hesitated for only a moment. "We're friends. Actually that's not true. I just met her, but our parents are friends. When things got crazy, she needed help."

The hotel room was standard—couple of beds with a nightstand between them, a dresser was under the wall-mounted TV. The woman in charge seemed very calm while her two men blocked the small hallway that led to the door.

"You knocked out one of my men upstairs." She looked at me suspiciously. "And even now you don't seem as scared as she is."

I shrugged.

She made a noise, almost like a hum. She sounded like a mom considering a response she didn't think was truthful.

Her air of cool cracked as someone banged on the door.

"Hotel security!" Dad's voice bellowed from the hall. "We have to clear the building."

"Move away from there," she said quietly to her men. "Sit on the bed and look casual. Don't be stupid." That final remark was directed at us.

She got to the door just as it opened. I couldn't see beyond her, though. She tried to block the view into the room.

"Thank goodness you're here." She sounded nervous. "What's happening?"

"We're evacuating the building, ma'am. Con Ed is here to figure out what's happened with the power and it's safer outside."

The cavalry was here! I made sure not to react, not even the slightest hint to Sofia.

"Now if you'll come with us, ma'am, we can lead you out."

"But I—" She gasped and moved back as Dad, along with two others, entered.

"I'm sorry. Everyone out—now. No exceptions."

The woman lost control of the situation as Dad kept barking out orders. He moved close to Sofia and me while the men he was with ushered the woman and her guys out.

"Come on, you two. Let's go." Dad lifted his arm and gestured toward the door. "Let's get you down to the street."

Sofia played along. I went first, and Dad put Sofia between us.

By the time we got into the hall, the guards who'd come in with Dad were out of sight with the people who'd captured us. "Stop," he said quietly as the door to the room closed behind us. We huddled around him. "Get to the other staircase. Opposite end of the hall. Up four flights. Your mom's at the door."

Neither of us had light. I'd lost track of my phone—either the woman had it, or it was somewhere in the room. I went back to having one lens on night vision since Dad illuminated the hallway with a big flashlight.

"Let's go." As I'd done so often in the past few minutes, I took Sofia's arm and brought her along with me. We didn't want to be on this floor if any of that woman's people came back.

We got to the staircase, and I went into full night mode. We moved carefully. I stayed behind Sofia with my left hand on her lower back and my right on the railing. She held the rail also as she climbed carefully but deliberately. I counted the floors and stopped us at the right door.

"Get behind me. Just in case." There was no one in the stairwell, and I had no reason to think Mom didn't have the situation under control, but better to be safe.

I opened the door a crack and got blinded by a burst of light. Quickly, I adjusted the lenses.

"Theo," Mom whispered, "come on."

I moved aside so Sofia could pass. Mom and I flanked her as we moved rapidly down the hall to a room with its door ajar. Mom waited until Sofia and I entered before coming in behind us and shutting the door.

"Thank God," Marcella said as Sofia went to her. Oliver joined them for a hug.

The room, identical to the one we'd been in downstairs, was illuminated by two lanterns, which cast strange shadows across the walls. The curtains were drawn, and since they looked like the blackout kind to let guests easily sleep past sunrise, no one would see our lights shining.

"You okay?" Mom asked quietly.

"Yeah."

Mom studied me in the low light. She watched me close

whenever I came back from something TOS related. It started when I got snatched off the bike last fall, and it hadn't changed in the months since. No matter how much of an agent she was, she couldn't shake being Mom.

"I'm really fine. Not even hurt." I lowered my voice further even though I was sure it would still travel. "She's a little shaken up, though." I gestured with my head toward Sofia. "But I don't think she's injured."

Mom nodded and pulled me into a hug, which I happily accepted and returned. "They're all a bit shaken right now."

"Are you okay? You kicked some butt down there."

That was the first time I'd seen Mom in action. While I had trained periodically with Dad and John, Mom had never taken part. To see her take down somebody tonight was kinda cool.

She chuckled softly as she nodded. We were on topics we probably shouldn't talk about in front of the Glenwood's. I'd steal some time with her later.

The lock clicked on the door, and Mom and I turned, adjusting our stance. I had to suppress a grin. I liked that we reacted in the same way at the same time. Just before the door opened there were rapid-fire taps against it. An identifying code that was private to the three of us—not even John knew it. We relaxed as Dad opened the door, stepped in quickly, and closed it.

"This hallway's clear." He looked to me. "You okay?"

I rolled my eyes at him. "That's all anybody asks." I smiled. "Yeah, I'm good. Thanks for the rescue."

"My pleasure." He pulled my phone from his pocket and handed it over. "Figured you'd want this back."

"Awesome. Thanks." I pocketed the device.

"The room's probably a dead end. We're pretty sure she broke in when she needed to use it because there were signs of forced entry. Subtle though it was. We're dusting for prints to see if we can get identification."

"So, they're in custody?" Oliver asked, not leaving his family's side.

"Yes," Dad came farther into the room. "The woman and two men who were holding them are in NYPD custody. They also have three of the four who invaded the ballroom. I'll be kept updated on what they find out."

"Thank you. Thank you all." Oliver sounded emotional. "I don't know what we would've done if you hadn't been here. My security guys were next to useless. And you"—he stepped to me and put his hands on my shoulders—"I don't know how you could see, but you kept Sofia safe, and I owe you for that."

I didn't know what I should say. I hadn't exactly kept her safe. I got us captured although it did work out in the long run. "You're welcome. If we have to do this again I'll try to avoid capture."

"Dude, I'd have been toast if it wasn't for you." Some of Sofia's swag reemerged, and it was good. "Even when they got us, you stayed chill." She looked between the adults in the room. "He talked to her real smooth. Like he knew it was all going to be okay."

"Thank you." Oliver squeezed my shoulders as Marcella stepped closer.

"Yes, thank you." She nudged her husband aside, so she could hug me. She held me for a few moments and then moved on to my parents. "You were all amazing tonight. I'd doubted Oliver's decision to bring in outsiders, but it was clearly the right choice. I've no idea how we're going to repay you all."

Dad hugged her back. "I'm glad we could help."

Dad's phone rang, and he pulled it from his pocket. It

suddenly dawned on me that he wore a hotel security uniform. How did he get that? Pretty amazing. The debriefing the three of us would have later would be interesting.

"Great. Thanks," he said into the phone. "We'll be right down."

"There's a car downstairs that will take us back to Brooklyn. It's in the hotel's loading dock."

"Good," Marcella said. "Let's go home."

NINE

Despite the excitement of last night and the debrief we had once we got back to the house, I was still up early. It was too ingrained for me to do otherwise. I did exactly what I would do if I was at home—worked out.

Since I was playing roller hockey, I'd brought skates with me. I shot a text to my parents to let them know Prospect Park was my destination. The morning had a cool edge to it, which felt so good—a slight reminder of the fall weather I liked so much. The sun was already up and it filtered through trees casting shadows. As I skated into the park, last night was on my mind.

Someone went to a lot of trouble to black out an entire building. The damage was bad enough that they didn't think the hotel's electrical system would be restored for a couple of days between sorting out the crime scene and repairs.

TOS was now officially involved. Dad contacted Lorenzo when I wasn't at the contact point and had him find my chip.

Having TOS on board would significantly speed up the

facial recognition analysis of everyone I captured with the lenses. I uploaded the images last night.

I surrendered to the skate and started up a pretty significant hill. It didn't occur to me to check the elevations before I went out. I'd assumed the park would be flat. But the hill became a righteous workout. I was glad I only went out in shorts and a T-shirt because I'd considered sweats to combat the coolness.

Hitting the top of the hill was a relief. I squatted down to keep my center of gravity low as I headed downhill. The speed provided a perfect mix of terror and awesomeness. I did another full lap and was satisfyingly exhausted when I returned to the apartment.

Just as I unlocked the door, my phone vibrated with Dad's text signal.

Come to the Glenwood's kitchen when you get back.

There must be news. I went in my apartment—it was still weird thinking of it that way—pulled off the skates and slipped on sneakers. I also grabbed a towel from the bathroom, so I could wipe off some of the sweat as I headed next door.

I knocked and tried the doorknob, but it was locked so I pressed the intercom button. The intercom sparked to life almost instantly.

"Hello?" It sounded like Christian.

"Hey, it's Theo."

A buzz sounded, and the door lock clicked. "Come on up."

Mom and Dad, Oliver, Marcella, and Sofia were all together, seated around the dining room table. Marcella talked animatedly about something while everyone else smiled and nodded. The families had merged, as if last night hadn't happened and today was a normal morning with everyone gathered for breakfast.

"Morning, Theo." Mom smiled. "Good skate?"

"Yeah. The park was pretty epic. I don't think I've ever gone that fast on blades. I wish I had my bike here because that loop through the park is great. So, what's up?"

"Please, join us for breakfast." Oliver held up his coffee mug and gestured to me.

"No thanks on the coffee," I said taking a seat next to Mom. "I'm more of a soda guy, or water."

Christian buzzed around the kitchen, and in short order there were four cans of soda in front of me to choose from. They even had Dr Pepper, which instantly made me like this family even more. Spread across the middle of the table, was an array of eggs, toasted bagels, bacon and some very flat, orange something I didn't recognize. A plate and silverware were handed to me, also from Christian, so I could dig in.

"It seems," Mom began, "that this may be about some sort of industrial espionage."

Last night was a distraction? But aren't there easier ways to manage that than going after the owner? Unless, instead of money, they wanted the Glenwoods to pay by handing over a company asset.

"At the same time the group made their move on us last night, there was an attempted hack on the Glenwood Music distribution system," Oliver said. "It controls everything from how music is mastered and then released to digital sellers, streaming services, radio stations and CD pressing plants."

"You said attempted. Your team was able to stop it?" This suddenly got a lot more interesting since apparently there were computer systems involved. "Was it inside or outside?"

"Outside. Our team caught it before any disruptions occurred." Oliver looked concerned but not freaked out, which I liked. Too often victims of a hack reacted in a knee-jerk way that caused more issues. "What I don't know is what they could gain from this."

"Is there any customer data in the system? Credit card details or anything like that?" Dad asked.

Sofia, who sat across from me, stayed quiet but looked intense as she seemed to pay close attention to the conversation.

"Theo, you really should eat." Marcella smiled at me. "This is serious but not serious enough to not eat."

"She's right," Dad added. "We'd mostly eaten our fill before Oliver got the email with this information."

I smiled as I served myself a little bit of everything. I was starved after the skate. "All right. Back to Dad's question. What kind of info can be taken from the MDS?"

Oliver detailed how the system worked as I ate. There wasn't any kind of customer data or way to access money. It held the library of music, encoded for each of the systems it distributed to, and kept a record of purchased downloads and streams.

"It seems like an innocuous system to go after." Dad looked thoughtful, as if trying to find the missing piece.

"Unless it's further smokescreen," Mom said.

"Let me focus on this system today." I looked between them and then landed my gaze on Oliver. "Do you have anyone trusted I can work with to analyze the attack?"

Oliver sighed and looked unsure. "I'll introduce you to our head of IT security today."

"Why the hesitation?" Dad asked. "If it's about Theo—"

"No," he said quickly. "It's not that. All of this makes me wonder who I can trust. Melissa's been with the company for a couple of years. I'm sure...."

"We didn't find any red flags on our first analysis of the employees yesterday. As we dig deeper today, we'll check her out first."

Oliver visibly relaxed at Dad's decision.

"And how will you be able to find anything?" Marcella asked, redirecting the conversation to me.

"I might not. But I can put in monitoring systems, that only I know about, to look at the network activity and perhaps catch anything that doesn't look right from the inside or out."

"You mentioned yesterday that you wanted to try to hack the system from the outside," Oliver said. "Is that still your plan?"

"Given what's happened, it's better if I go into more of a defensive mode and look for traces of how the breach happened to prevent another."

Oliver nodded, and he and Marcella shared a look.

Oliver fixed his gaze on my parents. "What do you two think of the strategy?"

Mom spoke first. "When it comes to computers or technology, I trust his judgment one hundred percent."

"In the meantime," Dad continued, "we'll look at the employees further and continue to question the people apprehended last night."

"How should we go about the day?" Marcella asked.

"As normal as possible," Mom said. "We don't want to give away to anyone that there's concern. We managed to keep the media focused on the power outage and away from the attempted abduction. There's no reason not to have a regular day. If anyone asks, just state the obvious. Yes, you were there last night. Yes, it's a shame the event was disrupted."

"I've got studio time booked today plus the live stream to release the new song tonight." Sofia spoke for the first time, and she sounded very businesslike. "Should we reschedule?"

Once again, Marcella and Oliver exchanged a look—this time of parental concern.

Mom stepped in. "Unless there's a business reason that you would cancel the performance, I say go forward. If you're inside the Glenwood building, you should be safe. The attempts so far have all been in public places where you're more exposed."

"Or, if you don't want to do it." Marcella looked at her daughter as she laid her hand over hers.

Sofia thought for a moment. "Let's do it. The song needs to get out there. It's bad enough those assholes disrupted a wonderful tribute." She put her hand over Marcella's. "Let's not delay this part of it. The performance is in our building with only fans in attendance, so it should be okay."

Marcella beamed at her daughter, and she gave a shyer smile in return. Sofia was impressive. The public persona I'd seen a little bit of didn't compare with how she behaved around her family.

"Theo, can you go with Sofia?" Marcella asked as she adjusted to hold Sofia's hand in hers. "Just to, you know, be there. Just in case."

I looked to Sofia. "I don't suppose the studio is in the same building as the distribution system and the IT team?"

"It is actually. We've got a few studios at headquarters."

"Then perfect."

"This streaming event. You said it was for fans only. What does that mean exactly?" Dad asked.

"Only people who RSVP'd in my Facebook fan group are admitted. And probably not all of them because of space limitations." Sofia shrugged.

"A couple of hours before the event, we tell people they can queue up outside the building," Oliver added. "And we'll cut the line at the capacity mark."

"This sounds risky," Dad said. "I assume this would be mostly teenagers, and we don't want to put any young people at risk."

Everyone was silent for a few moments, considering alternatives. The event was secondary to me as I wanted to dig into the computer systems.

"It's happening in a small theater inside the building. Everyone will go through security, and we can even preview the list ahead of time from the RSVPs."

"Theo's gonna be with me, so I feel completely safe." She smiled, and I felt like I'd been flirted with.

My face heated. I knew she paid me a compliment, but it made me uncomfortable and embarrassed.

"And look how cute he gets when he blushes." Sofia looked at me with a teasing grin.

I didn't know her well enough to know what kind of comeback to make. I just shook my head and tried to be exasperated. It didn't help that my parents giggled.

"Careful, he's got a boyfriend," Dad said.

Sofia raised her hands in surrender. "I wouldn't want to get in the way of that." She continued to eye me as a smile played across her lips.

That didn't reduce what I knew was a vivid red blush across my face.

"Okay." I pushed my empty breakfast plate away and

grabbed my half-empty can of Dr Pepper. "I'm gonna walk away before anyone says more. Give me a half hour to get cleaned up and my stuff together. That okay for you, Sofia?"

"Sure."

I turned to Mom and Dad. "I'll catch up with you later. Let me know if you find out anything useful, and I'll do the same."

"Will do." Dad clapped me on the back.

I wasn't sure what it was going to be like to spend the day with Sofia, especially if she made cracks that embarrassed me. This was definitely the weirdest mission yet.

TEN

As PLANNED, I spent the day at the recording studio with Sofia. Oliver hatched a plan to pass me off as an intern on an MIT project. It wasn't much of a stretch, of course, and it allowed him to easily ask one of his IT people to walk me through how the distribution system worked. Melissa Jones, Oliver's chief security officer, took me through how it worked from the moment a song file entered the system until it became publicly available to be downloaded or streamed. She seemed surprised by some of the deeper technical and security questions I asked, but she answered because Oliver granted me full clearance.

The recording studio, in some ways, was more comfy than our living room. Sure, there was the functional area with the huge control console which sat in front of the glass that separated the studio from the production and guest area. It was the space behind the engineer that was plush with couches, chairs, and places to relax. There was even a small kitchen area. You could, if you needed, live here for days. Which I guessed musicians did sometimes.

I carved out a back corner for myself. After taking over a

chair that had a side table as well as an ottoman, I switched back and forth between having the computer on my lap and using the ottoman as a desk.

Once Sofia's friends arrived, I was introduced as a friend from Boston. She didn't try to pass me off as someone she didn't actually want in the studio, which was cool because I'd thought she might try to make it seem like she'd been forced to bring me.

Oliver was in and out as the day went on. He was eager to see if I found clues. Nothing concrete surfaced by four, but I'd methodically gone through the system to increase the chance of not missing anything.

I wrapped up my analysis when Sofia sent her friends away, so she could prepare for the live stream. There were grumbles; a few people had expected to be allowed to stay. But Sofia held her ground and didn't try to placate her friends.

As they filed out, I put my stuff away, so I'd be ready to move to the theater.

"You've been pretty quiet today." Sofia flopped down onto the couch adjacent to the chair I was in. "What'd you find?"

"Nothing yet." I shrugged. "Do you always have as many people in here as you did today? It's not exactly good for security."

"I've known most of them since elementary school. There's no way they're caught up in any of the shit going on. You got friends like that, right?"

I scooped up my backpack and took a drink from the Dr Pepper I had. "If someone wanted to get to you, they might use your friends to do it. Like the ones who didn't want to leave, for example. I don't want to make you paranoid, but you should keep that in mind."

She scowled. I prepared for pushback, or maybe a celebrity-style tantrum, but it didn't come. Instead she nodded and looked sad. "I suppose you're right. I'll think about it." Her energy roared back a moment later. "Come on," she said, standing up. "I need to make sure everything's ready."

I followed, slinging my backpack over my shoulder as we headed into the hallway.

My phone rang with John's ringtone. It was the unsecured line.

"I gotta get this." I swiped the screen to connect the call as we got in the elevator. "Hey, John, this is a pleasant surprise."

"It is, yeah. I didn't plan on coming to New York, but I'm here now. I'm in the lobby of Glenwood Music, and I need someone to give me authorization to come up."

John was here? Interesting. I guess Mom or Dad asked him to come assist.

"Sure. One second, I can help you out." We got off the elevator and stepped into a very posh theater lobby. "Hey, Sofia, a colleague is in the lobby. Can you give the okay for him to come up?"

"How well do you know them? We can't let just anybody in, you know?" She gave me a smart-assed look.

"I deserve that."

"Yes, you do." She put her hand out for my phone, and I let her have it since it wasn't a secure call. She talked to lobby security, so John could get credentials.

I waited for John while Sofia went into the theater to talk to the technicians. A bartender set out sodas and snacks. This lounge space, which seemed a more appropriate term than lobby, opened into the theater that looked like it could be set up for multiple uses. In this case there were lots of places for people to stand as well as couches and seating areas on platforms along the perimeter of the room. There were only supposed to be a hundred people here, a lot smaller than last night's event.

I turned as the elevator opened and John stepped out along with one of the large security guys that I recognized from downstairs.

"Hey, John, good to see you." We fist-bumped.

"Is Sofia here?" The security guy looked around. "I need authorization to—" He looked at me and then my badge. "Actually, you'll do." He handed a badge to John. "Make sure you drop that off when you leave tonight."

John nodded, and the security guy left.

How did I have authorization to authorize? I looked at the badge I'd worn around my neck all day. It had my name on it, with *Theo* in bigger letters and my last name beneath in smaller type. There was a green stripe at the bottom.

"Let me see yours a sec." John handed his over. His name was in the same style as mine. The badge, however, was gray whereas mine was white. Apparently my access extended beyond IT information.

"One day here and you can already tell people what to do. I'm impressed." John smirked as he took the badge and put it around his neck. "I'm supposed to meet up with Oliver, so I get access to information about all his security people. But he was on the phone, so I decided to check in with you first."

Music started in the theater. I gestured for John to follow so I could keep watch on the person I was supposed to be guarding. Sofia was on the stage listening to the band and occasionally stopping them to discuss things.

I dropped my bag on a table. "I don't have much. The

distribution system is huge, and it's taking me time to work through it in detail. On first look though it was tight."

He nodded. "I heard your skills were on display last night."

"Little bit." I shrugged and stared off to the stage. "I got us caught, so it wasn't exactly my best moment."

"Things don't always work out like you want. You know that from the simulations you've been through. That it was okay in the end is sometimes all that really matters."

I looked at John. "I know. And I know if I wasn't there, Sofia probably wouldn't be on that stage now. But, I can't help that I want to be better."

John knocked his shoulder into mine. "Take it from someone who's been in this for a while—you're doing just fine."

"There you two are." It was Oliver, looking rushed. "You must be John. I'm sorry I didn't have the right badge for you downstairs. I just now got Victor's message that you were coming." He took a breath. "I'm sorry it's been a busy afternoon and I seem to have left my manners. Oliver Glenwood." They shook hands.

"John Keller. Nice to meet you. I was just catching up with Theo."

Oliver nodded but didn't pick up that conversation. He probably wanted to forget last night. He handed John a new badge and the green stripe was visible. "I understand you want to review all the company and personal security teams."

"Yes. Victor and Katherine thought I could help out on the personnel side of things."

"Happy to have you on board. My head of security has already discussed his concerns with me, and he's reviewed everybody over the past couple weeks. He's also offered his resignation since he feels responsible. You want to come up to my office and we can talk? I'm sure Sofia is about to crank up the volume in here."

John nodded. "That'll be fine." He looked to me. "We'll catch up later."

"I'll be down here until after the live stream is over."

John clapped me on the back and headed out with Oliver. I dropped onto the couch and watched Sofia do her thing. The band played the song from last night, which sounded even more amazing with the addition of strings. She sang softly, without a microphone, and moved around the stage as if thinking about what she wanted to do.

I pulled out my phone and tapped FaceTime to see if Eddie was around. In the middle of the afternoon, he could be any number of places, but I knew he was off work today. It only rang once before his face filled the screen.

"How's hanging with the stars?" He grinned at me. He was somewhere outside with blue sky filling the space around his head.

"Surreal."

"Where are you? There's music in the background and it's kinda dark."

"Let me show you." I flipped the camera so Eddie could see the stage.

"No way. You're at that live stream thing? I'm so jealous. You were with her last night, weren't you? I saw the news about the craziness."

I turned the phone back, so I could look at him. "Yeah." I tried to make it sound boring. "It was a snooze between the reception and the dinner. The music was good—and yeah, you heard that right. I liked the music. The whole power failure thing was just obnoxious. It took forever to get out of there."

"But you got to do it *with* them."

"Are you about to become my starstruck boyfriend?" I teased him because I still couldn't believe he followed celebrities like he did.

"Maybe. Just a little bit." He looked sheepish on the screen, and I wished I was with him to help wipe that look off his face. "How long's it take to get there?"

"Three-ish hours on the train."

"Damn. It'd be cool to be there with you. I guess I'll just have to settle for watching online."

I hadn't been paying attention to the stage where the music continued, so when Sofia plopped in next to me on the couch, I jumped.

"Sorry. Didn't mean to spook you." She looked me over and then sounded apologetic. "And I'm interrupting a phone call. Sorry."

"Is that Sofia?" Eddie practically squealed. "Right next to you?"

In nearly two years of going out, I never heard Eddie make a sound quite like that. I struggled not to laugh. He'd never forgive me if I embarrassed him in front of Sofia after all.

Sofia turned the phone toward her and waved. "Hi! You must be the boyfriend. You're very lucky, dude."

"Yes, I am." I didn't have to see Eddie to know he was working hard to control his excitement after that outburst. "I'm looking forward to the stream tonight. It sounds like the new song is pretty epic."

"That's what we're hoping for. I'll send Theo back with an autographed copy for you."

"That'd be amazing." Eddie drew out *amazing* into about ten syllables.

"Sofia!" Someone from the stage called out. "We're ready for you."

"All right, gotta get back to it. Nice meeting you, Theo's boyfriend." I turned the phone back toward me and saw his beautiful, grinning face. "You should come down front and stream this rehearsal just to him. It will be like you're here together for a sneak peek."

"You into that?" I knew Eddie's answer, but I asked anyway.

"Hell yeah." As expected the contorted look on his face told me I was crazy. "I might not be able to speak to you if you don't let me see."

I went down front but stayed far enough away from the stage so Eddie had the full view. Sofia did "Guardian" with the full band behind her. She also did a couple of other songs.

"That was so cool," Eddie said after it was over, and I had the camera back on me.

"Glad I could share it with you."

The wide grin on his face was adorable, and I badly wanted to kiss him.

"I should go."

"All right. Glad we got to hang for a bit. You're awesome. Call me later?"

"For sure. I love you."

"Love you too." We made kissy faces at the screen before he disconnected.

Sofia jumped off the stage and headed up the aisle, looking to me as she passed. "Wanna get a drink?" she asked.

I followed and found Sofia coming from behind the bar with two cans of soda—Coke and Dr Pepper. I met her at a couple of chairs that faced each other.

"My favorite." I took the soda and popped the top as we sat. "Thanks."

She took a long drink of her Coke Zero. "Can I ask you a question?" Her gaze was intriguingly piercing. In the limited time I'd spent around her so far, I'd seen many moods but not this one.

"Sure."

She leaned forward and further amped her seriousness. "I know you say you did what you did last night because it was what you needed to do. But there was more than that, you were calm and moved exactly like you *knew* what you were doing. Whereas me, I was scared out of my mind." She sighed and ran her hand through her long hair. "Don't get me wrong, the Central Park thing with Dad was scary, but last night it was dark and people chased us. I didn't know what to do. I couldn't see. But somehow there you were, guiding your dad to us and protecting me. Someone you don't even know."

We held each other's gaze. I couldn't read her look. A shrug seemed like the best response.

"I'm not sure I could do that for a stranger."

I chose my words carefully just like I do with Eddie. "We're here to help you guys, and I've been asked to lend a hand where I can. Most of that involves the technology. But it also means doing more if necessary. We are here to protect you and your family. It's that simple."

Sofia leaned back, her gaze making me slightly uncomfortable. Why was she scrutinizing me? Did she expect some other answer to miraculously pop out of my mouth?

"The gun scared me. I have friends who've been shot...."

"I've been through some stuff in the last year. And that includes being shot while protecting someone else. It's made me tougher I guess."

She sat back in her chair. "How'd that happen?"

I recounted the public story around the computer science competition back in the spring. Her mouth dropped open more than once. Maybe it was because the circumstances were unexpected, or she was surprised that I would go to such lengths to protect my classmates.

"I've also had the unfortunate experience of being abducted. I was snatched off my bike in the middle of the day, and it was the scariest thing ever. If I can keep that from happening to anyone else, I'll do it."

"Dude, I had no idea. I'm glad you're on my side—well our side."

"Sofia to the stage please," a voice called over the theater's PA system.

Sofia stood and offered me a hand up. I took it, and she pulled with such force that it brought me up right in front of her, face-to-face, with virtually no space between us. She was stronger than she looked.

"I was serious when I said that your boyfriend's very lucky." Her low, seductive voice reminded me of the girl-friend song Eddie'd played for me.

"I—"

"I hope I find someone like you some day." Her voice bounced back to normal. She let my hand go, grabbed her soda off the table and smiled before she took off into the theater. "It's good to know great guys like you exist."

ELEVEN

The next morning, I was with Sofia back in the studio as she worked. The live stream had been a huge success with thousands of viewers and positive feedback for the new music. She was in a good mood.

Meanwhile I focused on my analysis of the distribution system. Glenwood Music had solid technical systems and processes in place. Oliver had surrounded himself with good IT people. Even when I found an exploit, the system would cut my connection before I could do any damage. For employees with access, each action went into the logs for review if needed. The process provided maximum security.

When the engineer took a break, Sofia came over and sat down. "This weekend I'm shooting segments for a Christmas special. You and Eddie can be my guests."

As much as it'd be cool to take Eddie to something like that, I couldn't say yes without knowing if I'd have work to do. But man it'd be cool if he could visit. I balanced seeing him and work all the time. Maybe—

"Where'd you go?" Her hand waved in front of my face. "He seemed to love catching rehearsal last night so I thought it'd be cool if you could take him to the taping. Maybe wear that suit from the other night and make a night of it."

"Sorry. It'd be super cool to get him down here, but let's see if we can get the problems solved first. Otherwise, my weekend will be all work. It wouldn't be fair to bring him for that."

She shrugged and nodded. "So hurry up and finish, then," she said impishly. She bounced and gyrated in what could only be called a happy dance. "Kidding. Back to the grind for both of us. I need to listen to some tracks. You might even like some of these."

"What do you mean? I like your music just fine."

She snorted, which was the last thing I would've ever expected. I didn't know she had that kind of goofy sound inside her. "I almost believed that. I've seen how you look when some of my songs play. I saw you at rehearsal, and I caught you once last night during the show. It's not really your thing."

I needed to make sure I didn't reveal my thoughts out in the open like that. "I loved what you and your dad did for your mom—and the way it sounded last night with the orchestra was incredible. But yeah most of your other music just doesn't do it for me."

"It's okay." She didn't sound offended. "I know the lane my music's in. It sells, so that's good. But I can't deny there's a bit of sameness."

"And if it makes you happy," I offered, trying to go for a more upbeat route, "there's no reason why you should change."

"After years of deliberately not collaborating with Dad, writing that song with him was a great experience. The fusion of our styles worked really well. And I've got some songs—ones I wrote on my own—that will come out soon that are different."

She went over to the console and took a chair next to the engineer. I followed and leaned against the low cabinet behind them.

"All right," I said, "play me something you think I'll like."

She grinned. I'd done exactly what she wanted, and she wasn't hiding her glee about that. She worked the computer that was to one side of the engineer's console. In a few seconds, sounds of piano, strings, and drums filled the room. As a cello came into the arrangement, I liked it even more.

"There's a smile."

The melody was really good, and as Sofia sang her voice melded with the music as if she were another instrument. The fusion was beautiful. I could point to a handful of tunes that I had on a playlist for times I needed inspiration. This track would sit well on that list.

"It's really good," I said after the song finished.

"Gimme your phone, I'll give you an advance copy."

"Cool. Okay." I pulled my phone from my pocket, set it in safe mode and handed it over. Using a regular iPhone cable, Sofia connected it to the computer and transferred the song via the distribution system.

"I'm glad you like it." She passed the phone back to me once the transfer was done. "I'm trying different styles on the next album. Mom's song will be on that and this will too. Let's see what you think of this next one."

She handed my phone back before pulling up another song on the computer. This song was faster, but it also featured an orchestra.

My phone screeched with an alert.

Normally alerts just go to my watch with a vibration,

but this was more serious I tapped the onscreen acknowledgment to silence it.

"What the hell was that?" Sofia asked.

I accessed the security logs and swiped to get to the details on the alert. "Some sort of a security issue."

"What kind of phone is that anyway?"

"It's an iPhone," I said with a quick grin to Sofia and the engineer who looked ready to bolt if he needed to. "With a few modifications. It is my line of work after all."

Sofia came over and tried to look at the screen. I pulled it back from her view. She didn't argue but sat back in her chair.

"Do we need to call someone?" the engineer asked. "Are we in danger?"

"The phone picked up a potential hack."

I sent the logs from the phone to my computer, so I could read them more easily. Two events had happened simultaneously. The M4A song file Sofia put on the phone was compromised. The logs also indicated an audio threat of some kind from the sound that played in the studio, which made no sense.

"What's happening, man?" Sofia asked after I'd been quiet for a few minutes. "I don't like the intense look you've got."

I didn't look away from the screen. "Give me a minute. This is weird."

I was less worried about the infected M4A than I was with the audio alert. A file with malicious code was one thing, but something encoded in the audio was unusual. It was only triggered by the second song.

"Can you play that song again?" I looked to Sofia.

"Um, sure. But should we really be listening to music now?"

I brought my computer to the console and activated its microphone. Unlike my phone, which had Siri always listening, my computer wasn't set that way.

"Are you sure?" The engineer looked at me skeptically.

I nodded as I typed a few keys. "Go ahead."

He pushed Play, and it only took a few seconds before the computer and the phone flashed a warning message.

"You can stop."

He turned it off, and the alert disappeared. Going back to the logs, there were no details on what the threat was, only that there was something unknown in the audio.

"Man, what is it? Talk to us." Sofia was over my shoulder again, and even though this was technically TOS software, she wouldn't get any sensitive information looking at the screen.

"There's malicious code in the M4A file you put on my phone, but there's also something in the audio of what you just played."

"Is that even possible?"

How could she ask that? She heard the same alarms I did. And I wouldn't say it if it wasn't true.

"Can I see your phones a second?" I looked between Sofia and the engineer.

They both looked anxious but handed them over. There was nothing on the devices that looked out of place and even the scan I did with the computer came back clean.

"You said you were giving me an advance copy, so this isn't public yet?"

"A couple radio stations have preview copies to play. It doesn't go on sale for another few days. This is a new version because I wanted the strings bumped up. You might be the only one that has it."

"What version went to the stations?"

"Yeah," the engineer said. "Radio has this one." He clicked on the computer and the song started again. Even I could hear the difference in the strings. No alerts popped up.

I reached for the connector cable and plugged my phone in. "Send that one to my phone."

He nodded as he typed.

No warnings after the file loaded either. I went into the music player and tapped play. The song started and still no issues. Whatever had been done to alter the file happened after the new copy was made.

"I need to talk to your dad and my parents." I closed my laptop and grabbed my pack. "You gonna be okay here?" I asked Sofia. "I'll be back as soon as I can."

"Oh, I'm coming with you. I want to hear about this."

TWELVE

After I briefed Oliver, Sofia, and my parents, my role on the case expanded. We needed to get to the bottom of what was in this file and why it triggered security measures.

Until John returned to the Glenwood office, I still needed to keep an eye on Sofia too. I fired up my phone as a secure hotspot to connect to the TOS network and work with Lorenzo.

Mom, Dad, and I also went on comms to simplify communication. We weren't leaving them open to all of our chatter, but at least we'd be able to talk easily if we needed to. I wore the contact lenses too because it'd be a good test of the improvements we made in transmitting and recording a computer screen. In earlier versions the text appeared blurry.

First thing I uploaded to TOS were the files along with my notes.

Working with audio files was outside my expertise, but sifting through the raw code, compression algorithms, metadata and other file components was fascinating. It was easy to see differences in the files. Some of that was because the song itself changed, but the file was larger too, and that had to be due to the inclusion of code that didn't belong. I discovered a compact piece of code designed to transmit data. While the transmitter was obvious, how it lifted the data from the device wasn't. I'd need more time on that.

The audio component remained a mystery. I've never known a TOS phone to go off over a song, even though the phone was always listening. I tasked the TOS team with finding out if there were any similar cases.

I put my earbuds in and played the file on the laptop. Nothing stood out. I didn't have any sound tools but the engineer definitely did. Maybe he could discover something.

When Sofia stopped playing to scribble something on the paper on a music stand in front of her, I asked the engineer to call Sofia in.

She wasted no time. "Did you find something?"

"There's a virus buried in the file, but I still can't account for the audio alert. You mentioned you had the song remastered, but did you hear anything wrong with the new version?"

"No. Danny, did you?"

He shook his head. "It sounded like I'd expect once the encryption was added. I finished the mix this morning and submitted it to be mastered. We played that version."

"Do you have a copy of the file before you sent it for the mastering?" I asked.

"Of course. We keep all the source files so we can go back to the raw material if we need to make changes, like adjusting the strings." Danny used the computer Sofia had used earlier to open up new files. In short order we listened to the song again. This time no alerts occurred.

"Can you display the soundwaves for both versions?"

"Sure can. One sec." Danny worked at the keyboard and also turned on another monitor that was over the console. Two graphs displayed and they were nearly identical. "On top is the original and below is the M4A."

"Can one of you—"

"What is that?" Danny asked before I could finish. "This line." He stood and pointed out a portion of the pattern. "How is there a straight line that runs through the entire song? Let me see if I can isolate that."

Sofia and I looked at each other, and she shrugged. Keys, my former mentor who was killed on a mission earlier this year, would've loved this case. She was so into music and would've been all over the graphs.

Danny played the song and removed parts of the tune. As he did, the graphs changed until most of the music was gone, but there was still a line indicating there wasn't complete silence.

"I don't hear anything," I said after straining to listen.

Danny grabbed headphones off his console, pushed a couple buttons, and put them on. After a few moments he shook his head and handed them off to Sofia.

"I can't hear anything either."

We both looked to Sofia.

"It's silence." She removed the headphones and laid them on the console. "If I didn't know you were playing something, I'd assume you forgot to push the button."

"And this isn't in the original file?"

"No." He pointed to the screen again. "You don't see anything here that represents that line. It must be in a range we can't hear, but it registers on the graph because it's actually present."

"But how does your phone hear it?" Sofia asked.

"Siri, Alexa, all of them, listen to more than what

humans can hear as part of speech recognition. Play that"—I pointed at the screen—"over the speakers."

It only took a couple of seconds for the phone to react. Danny turned it off as soon as it did.

"Can you give me a file that has just that on it?" That would give us something to analyze without the rest of the song.

"Sure, if you think it'll help I'll render it now." Danny typed. "Why would someone add something like this to a song?"

"I honestly don't know. This is new to me. We need to keep this quiet for now, so, other than Oliver and my parents, this information can't leave the room."

Sofia and Danny both nodded.

Just as we wrapped up, some musicians and a couple of Sofia's friends arrived. I retreated to my corner. Danny loaned me an extra set of headphones, so I could listen more closely while running the analysis. The first thing to do, however, was get in touch with Lorenzo, so I opened a secure text window. I needed a sound expert.

Hi, Doc. I need to chat when you're free. Can't call because can't identify on the phone right now. Please call when you can.

I connected to my home computer because I wanted more processing power than I had on the laptop. I put my analysis tools to work to deconstruct the binary code of the file in the hopes it would identify the rest of the virus that I couldn't see.

Lorenzo rang my phone.

"Winger, Dr. Possible here."

"Thanks for calling me back, Doc."

"You actually caught me away from the computer. What's up with my celebrity security guru?"

I groaned.

"Sorry, I couldn't resist." I could hear him grin. "I saw that you uploaded some files. What'd you find?"

"Yeah. There's definitely an attack happening here." I got my earbuds from my pack, so I could plug in and have my hands free for the keyboard. Once I was connected, I caught him up. Some of it I typed in the chat window because I didn't want to reveal too much since the room had filled up with more of Sofia's friends.

"Wow," Lorenzo said once he was fully up-to-date. "Getting personal information stolen because you buy a song is significant on its own. The audio tone is something new and disturbing, though."

"Right? I can't imagine what it would be used for, or if it's being used now and I haven't figured it out yet. There's no indication anything executed."

"There are all kinds of safeguards built in to make sure phones don't react to an unauthorized sound. But it registered a threat. I'll get our team responsible for that function to review this. I think IT needs to be more involved in this case now."

"Agreed. I'll inform—" I had to edit myself. I couldn't say codenames because there were too many people around. "I'll authorize it and make sure the right people are notified."

"I'll let the team here know you're leading and on the scene for IT. Defender and Snowbird continue to command the overall mission," Lorenzo said.

"I'll continue to analyze."

I also typed a message to Lorenzo: *We should get Split Screen on this. Her abilities could be useful since she's shown an aptitude for uncovering mysterious things in code.*

There are functions triggered by these files that she might figure out.

It'd only been a few months since I'd turned down taking a full-time leadership position, but I still made suggestions.

"Good call on Split Screen. I'll let her know."

"Great. Once you get the team figured out, I'll set up a briefing for them."

"Sounds good." Lorenzo's typing provided the background noise to our talk. "Let me know if you need any support from me or if you need more resources. Since you're on the ground there, I understand your time might be split."

"Within the next couple hours, IT tasks will have my full attention."

"Great. I think I'm going to work on the sound file as well. I'm fascinated by that. It'll be more interesting than writing reports."

Reports sucked. I hated them and appreciated how much Lorenzo wanted a justifiable distraction.

THIRTEEN

A COUPLE OF HOURS LATER, Sofia took a break and came with me to Oliver's office since she wanted to stay informed. Dad was upstairs with him, and we got Mom and Marcella on a conference call since Marcella was at her office.

"I don't have any more than I did earlier. I've turned the information over to my colleagues so we can get to the bottom of it faster."

"Good call," Dad said. Luckily no one asked who my colleagues might be.

"Agreed," Mom added. "This would line up with the corporate espionage theory? Competitors perhaps?"

"It's certainly a possibility," Oliver said. "If word gets out about this, it could damage Glenwood Music. It could also cause issues for the entire industry if people don't feel they can trust the music they buy."

"And this ties back to the threat indicating it was the music distribution system the people targeting Oliver and his family were after," Dad picked up.

"Why pick Glenwood Music?" Mom asked. "They've

got a couple of high-selling artists, but they're still relatively small compared to other companies."

When had Mom become such an expert in the music business? She rattled off more statistics about the industry like she'd known it forever. It was clear where her focus had been in the past day or so.

"There are a lot of possibilities," Dad said. "If you target a smaller company first you can test out your plan. Once it works, you spread it to larger companies."

Oliver's expression was grim. "Should we warn people that possibly some of our music is infected?"

"We need to figure out if there are any other compromised song files in your repository." I looked to Oliver. "The song we know is infected hasn't been released yet. I'll write a search program that can scan the other files and tell us if there are any out there. That'll help us decide what to do."

"That's the critical first step," Dad said. "We need to know what we're dealing with and if it's out in the market now. We should avoid going public with any news. We don't want to tip our hand too soon."

"Okay. Obviously you have full access to anything you need. Anyone that you need to talk to or work with. If you get any pushback, come directly to me. Theo, do you need anything special?"

"I think I'm good."

Oliver nodded and looked around the room as if trying to make sure no one else was in his office. He dropped his head into his hands and wasn't the confident entrepreneur, media mogul I'd seen in action the past few days. "I really hope you're able to find the problem and the people behind it."

"We'll do everything possible." I looked to Dad. "I need

to work on this exclusively and for ease of access I should do it from IT. We need someone else with Sofia."

"I'm already on that." He gave me a subtle smile. "John's off-site but on his way back. He'll keep her safe."

"Exactly what I was thinking."

Oliver looked between us as if he didn't quite know how to react to the exchange we'd had, but he kept quiet about it. "Ask Christian to set you up with an office in IT and to make sure you get whatever you need from Melissa."

I looked forward to unraveling this complex situation.

FOURTEEN

THE AFTERNOON TURNED into a blur as I put the search in place to look for songs that were already infected and worked with the team Lorenzo assigned to analyze the files we had.

"I know you've had limited time to review our systems." Melissa sat across from me in my temporary office. "Do you see any way for someone on the outside to gain access? Our access logs only show the attempts you made when you first started as well as the one attack that occurred during the charity event. Beyond that we only see the regular traffic you'd expect."

"I tried a few different ways to get in, and the security was tight. I haven't had time to force my way in, but I don't believe I'd have an easy time of it between your automated systems and the security team." She nodded but still seemed apprehensive. "How many people overall have access to the system?"

She picked up the tablet from the desk in front of her and tapped out some commands. "There's only a couple dozen, and they either directly handle the distribution of music or pull reports. Those with access to reports don't handle the actual music files."

I nodded and thought for a moment. "We should get that list up to my dad and Oliver since they're vetting people to see if there's any possibility this is an inside job."

"I'll send it right now." She focused on the tablet, no doubt to send the email.

Melissa ran a tight ship. The security protocols were higher than what I would've expected to see from a corporate system without e-commerce directly tied in. Since the system handled file encoding, it provided the ideal point to add something to the song before it was released and it would be unlikely anyone would catch it before it got out.

"You really think it could be someone here?" she asked when she finished typing.

I looked up from my screen. I'd been working for an hour to deconstruct the infected file before Melissa stopped by. "It's very possible. An insider would have the knowledge how files are assembled and the best time to add additional encoding. If not an insider doing the actual work, an insider providing the access is possible. Speaking of, how often do you make employees change their passwords."

"We're on a forty-five-day cycle and people hate it."

I smiled and chuckled. When I started at TOS I was surprised they had a ninety-day refresh policy. While the IT team at the time appreciated my recommendation for a thirty-day cycle, it took a long time to get that implemented because it meant people had to learn a new password so frequently. It was one of the reasons we switched to fingerprints and retina scans as quickly as we could. They were easier than remembering the more complex passwords and passphrases we demanded.

"You're already ahead of the curve, then," I said as she

nodded. "What about access? Can people log in from outside the company network?"

"You have to log in to the network and then access it from your personal dashboard."

"How disruptive would it be if you cut off the access via VPN so that—"

"There's an extra layer of control in place." I loved that she anticipated where I was headed.

"Exactly." A chime sounded from my laptop and a notification popped up that one of my analyses was done.

"What is it?" she asked.

"My analysis of the first batch of songs is complete. There are anomalies." I called up the results and found three hundred and thirty-two files featured characteristics of the infected file I'd first seen.

She obviously saw my frown. "Can you tell me or does it just need to go to Mr. Glenwood?"

I pulled out my phone and dialed Dad on his regular line. He picked up quickly. "Theo, have you found something?"

"Yeah. Is Oliver with you?"

"Yes, he is. I'll put you on speaker."

"I'll do the same. I'm here with Melissa."

I put the phone on the desk.

"So, tell us." Dad wasted no time starting the briefing.

I told them about the findings. The scripts I ran went backward through the system, starting with songs that were to be released in the coming days and then back through the past month.

"I've just sent this list to the three of you so you can look it over."

Melissa visibly steeled herself. It only took a moment before her tablet pinged with the email.

"This is a disaster." Oliver spoke first. "This appears to affect our entire release slate for the next three weeks. It's a busy time for us as we're rereleasing a section of my back catalog as well as albums from several of our biggest artists. It's the start of the company's fifteenth anniversary. Not to mention the song Sofia and I did."

"So, you don't normally release this much?" Dad asked.

"No. At most it's usually one or two albums a month along with some singles. It can be a couple more if either of our two specialty labels release, but those are usually once a quarter."

"With the anniversary, a lot of publicity has happened around these releases?" I asked, curious about how many potential downloads they expected.

Oliver surprised me with a chuckle. "We must be doing something wrong because you are in one of our primary demographics."

"I'm often told my tastes are not exactly in the mainstream."

"Well," Oliver said, "we'll see if we can broaden those tastes once this is done. To answer your question, we're projecting more than a million downloads in the first week for 'Guardian' and then in the hundreds of thousands for new releases and more in the tens of thousands for releases."

"Back to our issue, when were these songs processed?"

"Melissa, do you have that data? All I know is they would've had to be in the system in time for any early promotions."

Oliver barely had the question asked before Melissa was working her tablet.

"The songs went into the system over a three-week period starting about six weeks ago." Her speech was peppered with pauses as she read the information. "Each file was initially processed within hours of its upload as expected, but the final processing date.... This doesn't make sense. The logs indicate each of these was reprocessed two days ago."

"Why would a large batch of songs be reprocessed like that? How did we not see that before?"

"What are the circumstances a file would be reprocessed?" Dad asked.

"Adding metadata—final artwork, final songwriting or producing credits, any last-minute changes like that. And we keep track of when those are done. I could see, for example, ten or fifteen songs all from the same album updated at one time for the final cover art."

"Do we know who made the bulk updates?" I asked.

Once again she tapped her screen. The scowl on her face grew the more she tapped.

"The updater information is missing." Disappointment sounded through her voice.

There was silence as the impact of that sunk in for everyone. Whoever did this not only had access but also the ability to cover it up.

"Since we've got the time stamps these changes happened, we should be able to work with the access logs to determine who was logged in at the time."

"Let's get that figured out," Oliver said. "I'm going to have Larson oversee the fixes. Theo, if you find any more, pass the info to Christian so he can send them on."

"We've got ten days before these go out, right?" Dad asked.

"To the general public, yes," Oliver answered quickly. "However, some of the songs can be accessed early by fan club members and reviewers. You need special codes to access them, and they can only be played on the website, with no downloads allowed until they go on sale. We do that to build buzz while mitigating piracy ahead of the release."

"There's potentially significant risk even in that setup. Depending on how the viruses are constructed they might be able to make the jump from the browser to the device. Let me test that right now. Can I get the URL of one of those sites so I can see what happens?"

"I'll have that sent to you," Oliver said. "Do you really think that's occurring?"

"Given the sophistication I've seen so far, I'd have to say yes." There was no reason to soften the blow.

Across from me, Melissa typed furiously on her tablet. On the phone I heard muffled talking from Oliver asking someone to get me the website info. While I waited, I created an area on my computer where my security tools could run on a browser and contain any damage the virus might cause.

Melissa looked up from her tablet. "Looking at the figures since these files were updated, the most plays for a song was fifty-four times and the least was ten. From my quick cross reference, these are available only to reviewers and haven't gone out to fan clubs yet. There's still three days before club release."

At least it was minimal distribution considering the number of songs that had the potential to cause damage.

"I've loaded one of the review sites. I'm going to play the song on mute." I clicked the settings for the audio. "Since we don't know the true intention of the strange audio we discovered in Sofia's track we must be cautious. Stand by."

I clicked play. The clock on the player started, and it was only a few seconds before my security panel popped open, indicating the computer would've transmitted data if

I hadn't quarantined the browser. The song also contained the mystery audio.

"I'm afraid this track is compromised. I'm going to set up some tracers along with fake data to see if I can find out where it's going."

"I'm going to have the site shut down temporarily. We can't—"

"I don't know if that's the best idea," Dad interrupted.

"But we have to—"

"How fast can the songs be replaced?" I jumped in. "We know the root files don't carry the viruses, or at least Sofia's didn't. If we're able to put out clean versions it might buy us time to do the necessary trace."

"We could also make it appear the song hasn't been updated," Melissa added. "If anyone checked the system they would think the infected file is still in place."

I nodded at Melissa for, again, finishing my thoughts.

"Okay," Oliver said reluctantly. "If we get that done in the next couple of hours, the review sites can stay up." I couldn't imagine what scenarios played out in his mind with this attack on his business. "Melissa, work with whoever you need to to get a list of who listened to the infected files. I'll work with PR and legal to determine how we want to reach out to them."

We all had tasks, so it was time to get back to it. "I'll update as soon as I have something new. Is there anything else to discuss?"

"I think that's it," Dad said.

Melissa nodded, and I told Dad we'd talk later.

"If you need anything, you know where my office is." Melissa left, and I sent updates to the TOS team.

FIFTEEN

I'd stayed at Glenwood Music until after nine and caught a ride back to Brooklyn with Dad and Oliver.

"So the data that's stolen is going to a location in Manhattan?" Oliver asked as he drove.

"That's what the trace shows. Although I would've expected it to go somewhere farther away, most likely overseas. It doesn't make a lot of sense. Once we're home, I've got a meeting to get updates from my colleagues."

"You're pretty amazing." Oliver stole a look at me in the rearview mirror. "You and Katherine raised him well, Victor."

"He's a good kid for sure. But where his computer stuff comes from, I have no idea because neither Katherine nor I think anything like he does."

My cheeks heated, and I was glad the inside of the car was mostly dark.

"Don't hesitate to contact me at any point if you need resources from the company, Theo. I'll make sure you get what you need no matter the hour. Victor told me you work late at night sometimes, I'll email you my personal cell that I keep at the bedside in case you need to reach me."

"I appreciate that."

I expected to be up late shuffling through what I'd get from Lorenzo so it was possible I'd need something. Hopefully I wouldn't have to wake him, though.

As we arrived in front of the house, one of the security men came out from the first-floor apartment they used as their base. Another staffer came and took the car away. I'd seen this play out a couple of times now, and I still marveled at valet parking at home.

As we got out, Sofia came down all bouncy and excited. What had her so enthusiastic?

Without stopping to say hello to her dad, she stopped in front of me. "Theo, man, great timing. I've got a surprise for you."

"That wasn't necessary." I tried to not be annoyed. "Plus, I've got a lot of work to do."

Oliver joined us as the car departed behind us.

"What's this, Sofia?" I wasn't skilled at reading Oliver yet, but he didn't look happy about the idea of a surprise. "This isn't some game we're playing. What Theo and his family are doing is critically important. I'm sure the surprise can wait until a more appropriate time."

Since I had a view of the front door, I saw John step into the doorway. Was he staying in the main house since the rest of us were in the guest apartments? It would certainly put him in close proximity to Sofia, although it seemed unlikely that she'd be in danger inside the house.

Defender, Snowbird, Winger, Shotgun here. Sofia brought Eddie here. He just arrived. I'm not supposed to tell you this, but I'm sure she's down there saying something about this big surprise she's got.

It took all the training that I'd ever had about the use of comms—along with a lot of self-control—to not show shock.

This would get messy quick. I had work to do, and I couldn't let Eddie distract from that. I could be in the open to a certain degree. It'd be easy to say I was consulting for the Glenwoods.

But he's here!

Excitement flooded me despite the inconvenience his arrival posed. It mixed with irritation that she'd done this despite our conversation earlier.

"You really need to take a few hours," Sofia said, excitement undeterred. "Didn't you say you had colleagues working with you? That gives you some time, right?"

"You know this is what I do, right?" My frustration seeped out further. "It doesn't always follow regular business hours. And I can't just abandon my team either."

"Whatever," Sofia said dismissively. "Come on." She grabbed me by the hand and pulled me with her. It was the reverse of when I moved her along at the hotel. I stole a look behind and found Dad and Oliver following.

"I already knew John was here." I forced Sofia to stop as we entered the house. "Hey, John." I held up my fist and he bumped it.

"He's not the surprise." Sofia tugged like a child eager for her parents to come downstairs for Christmas morning. "So smart, but so dense sometimes too."

We went upstairs to the living room level. Sofia made a big flourish once we got there so that my gaze would follow.

"Oh my God, Eddie! What're you doing here?"

I ran toward him as he stood up from the couch where he'd been chatting with Marcella. We hugged. Playing out a happy reunion was required—but also so easy. God, I missed him.

"Who's this?" Oliver asked as he crossed the room to Eddie and me.

"Oliver this is my boyfriend, Eddie Cochrane. Eddie this is—"

"Oliver Glenwood," Eddie interrupted, sounding reverent. "It's a pleasure to meet you, sir. I've loved your music, well, sort of forever."

"Good to meet you, Eddie." Oliver showed none of the annoyance he had when we were downstairs. "You have an amazing man here."

I really wasn't used to so many compliments. It felt good, but man it made me uncomfortable.

"Yes, sir, I'm well aware of how awesome Theo is." He took my hand, squeezed and didn't let go.

"What are you doing here? How'd you get here?" It was the question of the hour. The answer probably didn't matter since I'd have to manage him—like I always did. He was totally worth the extra effort. I couldn't suppress a grin.

"I got a Facebook message from Sofia. I didn't think it was really her. You know, why would she message me? Anyway, she invited me to come down to see her shoot a Christmas special this weekend. She said you were working —which by the way is very cool—but that you were okay if I came down."

And at least he knew about the work. Part of me relaxed. Given the celebrity status of this client, he might even encourage me to work.

"He can hang with me while you're working," Sofia jumped in, "But hopefully you two can find some time to hit the town too and then the taping on Saturday."

Dad and Oliver glared at her. No one thought this was a good idea.

Still. He was here. I made it work in Denver when he showed up and we had an amazing time. I'd find a way to make the most of this visit.

SIXTEEN

AFTER A NIGHT where I worked until two, Eddie and I still stole away around six thirty for a run in Prospect Park.

Eddie had stayed in the main house last night. Sofia played new music for him and kept him occupied while I worked with the TOS team. We'd made progress on the virus's capabilities and on a method to clean infected songs. Further traces also found that the data wasn't staying in Manhattan. It moved multiple times and part of the team worked on enhanced tracking.

"That was a good run. I can't believe you skated down that one hill, though," Eddie said. "I would've been terrified."

"There was a little bit of scary, but it was way fun. You'd love it. You're the one who loves roller coasters after all."

"I'm all strapped in for a coaster, which is very different from being on some tiny wheels." Eddie stole glances at me as we jogged along the sidewalk on the park's perimeter. "I'm glad I'm here, even if we can't spend all day together."

"I'm sorry about that."

"Don't be. I should've checked with you and not just accepted that Sofia said it was okay. I promise I'll stay out of the way."

"And I'll do my best to get this wrapped up so we can check out the city."

We were a block away from the house when my phone repeatedly chirped with text messages from multiple sources—Mom, John, and Lorenzo among them. I ignored the phone since I'd soon have privacy to check them. We found Mom and Dad headed for the Glenwood's as we arrived.

"Uh-oh," Eddie said quietly. "All those chirps weren't good news, were they?"

"Probably not."

"Good timing." Dad looked to me as we fell into step next to them. "Oliver's asked to see us."

I nodded, pulling out my phone to silence the alerts.

"What's going on?" Eddie asked.

"Not sure yet." Dad focused on Eddie. "It'll probably be best if you give us some privacy when we get in there. I'm not sure if he'll want to share the news."

"Of course." Eddie didn't miss a beat. "I should get cleaned up anyway."

As we got upstairs we heard a news broadcast.

"Big trouble this morning at a listening party hosted by a radio station in Atlanta. Multiple fights broke out and the scene turned violent. Police are on the scene of this breaking story, and we're joining a live broadcast from our Atlanta affiliate."

In the living room, John, Oliver, Marcella, Sofia, and Christian watched.

"We're here," Mom said as we joined them.

Eddie squeezed my hand and smiled before he continued up the next flight of stairs.

Sofia looked horrified while Oliver was as distressed as I'd ever seen him. Marcella seemed transfixed by the scene as they replayed cell phone footage of the incident while the reporter talked.

I recognized the song in the background. It was one we'd identified and cleaned yesterday.

The repetitive beat was unimaginative. It was gonna be an earworm most of the day.

Why was I tapping my foot to the beat?

Pain—no, irritation—crawled over my brain.

I scratched at my left ear and then rubbed my hand across my head.

If I could've scratched my brain directly I would've. It was like there was a bug just under my scalp.

How long were they going to play this song?

The music wasn't even that loud, but it was all I could hear.

"Theo," Oliver said, "I thought all these songs got cleaned yesterday and redistributed."

"What?" I snapped back. "Yeah. This is one we fixed."

"Are you okay?" Mom asked, touching my arm.

"Get off." I shrugged, shoved her hand away, and stepped back.

Why did I do that?

"What's gotten into you?" Dad asked.

Everybody stared.

"Nothing. Nothing." I turned to go downstairs. "I need to get to work. Figure out what's happening."

The phone vibrating in my pocket felt like it was trying to burrow into my leg.

"What the hell?" I struggled to pull it out.

I threw it hard to the floor, but the vibration continued. The noise was so loud between that and the damned song.

"Theo!" John grabbed me by the forearm and pulled me to him. "This isn't like you."

I grabbed his wrist and tried to force him to let my arm go. He hung on and grunted as I twisted with a maneuver he'd taught me. He finally let go, and I bolted, even though I wanted to hurt him worse.

"Leave me alone!" I roared.

"Everything okay down here? Theo?"

Eddie's voice didn't stop me. Moving too fast, I tripped on the stairs but righted myself before I fell. Several people yelled my name. The song, however, wouldn't get out of my head. It was like I was still upstairs.

Outside the song stopped as the door closed behind me. Halfway down the front stairs, I stumbled again and sat down hard.

What just happened?

We watched the TV. Something happened in Atlanta.

"Theo, are you all right?"

I looked behind me, and Mom was there with everyone else, including Eddie.

Dizziness made it hard to focus. I wanted to lie down. Sitting wasn't easy for some reason.

"What did I do?"

"We're hoping you could tell us." Mom sat next to me and I leaned into her.

"I feel like I've been... I don't know." This shouldn't be such a struggle. "It's like waking up from surgery."

"We should get him upstairs." John had a quiet urgency in his voice. "Whatever's going on we shouldn't deal with it out in the open."

That was John. Always practical.

"Can you stand?" Mom again.

I didn't want to move. Leaning against Mom was really nice. But John was right. We needed to go inside and figure this out.

"I'm not sure."

"Come on Theo." Dad was next to me and reached under my shoulder. "I've got you." I'd forgotten how strong he was. He pulled me up and my legs actually cooperated.

"Take it easy. One step at a time." Dad's voice remained calm, collected.

I didn't like being out of sorts—that's one of the things that kept me away from alcohol and drugs. More than a fuzzy brain, though I felt like my energy'd been zapped.

John came to my other side and made sure I didn't waver.

We got back inside. Oliver's security man stood guard at the door, and Christian kept watch too.

"Let's go in here." Oliver gestured to the first-floor sitting room.

They sat me down on a couch. I fell back into the cushions, happy I didn't feel the need to lie down anymore. So many awful sensations rolled through my head. The tingling was like pins and needles.

"What can you tell us?" Dad sat next to me. I hated being the reason all these people looked so concerned. The room was overcrowded. At least Glenwood's security stayed in the hallway.

"I'm not sure. As soon as we were upstairs it felt like something... this is going to sound crazy. There was like an itch on my brain and I couldn't hold back. I wanted to hurt John and both of you. It stopped when I couldn't hear the TV anymore."

"Is it possible that whatever happened to the people in

Atlanta affected you through the TV?" Mom asked. "How much do we know about the music they played?"

"We played some of those songs yesterday. I didn't freak out like this."

"What about that extra sound that you found?" Mom asked. "Could that have been dormant?"

"I suppose it's possible. So far that's baffled... the people analyzing it. If the master files were used to create new ones, it shouldn't be there. The scans I did on the clean versions were all clear."

"How did the radio station play the wrong ones?" Oliver asked.

"Maybe they didn't get the update?" Mom said.

It seemed impossible that a sound I didn't know I heard could make me, or anyone, get violent. Although there were many things about sound that I didn't understand.

"But why just me? None of you were affected."

Nobody spoke for a few moments, but it was Mom who finally broke the silence. "We'll have to do some research." She looked between Oliver and Marcella. "If violence can break out when these songs play, we've got to make sure it's not available."

"Agreed," Oliver said. "As much as it pains me from a business standpoint we have no choice but to shut down the distribution system and the preview sites."

"What about the music that's already out?" Dad asked.

Oliver shook his head. "They have the option to download updates if they're available, but once they've got it, they own it."

"We need to get that file from Atlanta." I tried to stand but was unstable. I fell back to the couch with Mom's guidance. "Dammit," I said quietly.

"I know you want to get back to this, Theo." Mom left

her hand on my arm. "But you're still recovering from whatever happened. And we have to be sure that you're not affected again. I'm not sure how you can work on it. You may not be able to have it on mute while you do the analysis."

"We've got plenty of noise-canceling headphones that will block any outside noise." Oliver walked over to a small cabinet that held a tiny music system on top. He opened it and pulled out a pair of headphones similar to what I'd seen in the studio.

"Okay," Mom said. "We need to keep everyone safe."

"I need to make some calls." Dad stood but before he left he leaned in and squeezed my shoulder. His gaze warmed and calmed me. He was always great at that and even in the midst of all this he managed to do it with that one look.

"I need to make calls too," I said. "I need to get some audio experts on the case."

"Can we really afford to open this up to still more people?" Oliver asked.

"Theo consults with authorized, trusted individuals. Victor and I can attest to that."

"Okay. I had to ask."

"Of course." I nodded.

Struggling to keep my balance, I stood.

"Shouldn't you rest like your mom said?" Eddie asked. He'd been studying me, behind the adults. He must wonder what he'd gotten himself into. "Maybe at least some breakfast to get your strength back?"

"There's no time for that." I regretted the frustration in my voice, but this was important and he should know that.

I needed to talk to Lorenzo so we could decide who

should be added to the team since the threat proved worse than we'd imagined.

"Eddie's right." What was Mom even saying right now? "Get some breakfast first." Her expression told me to roll with it. She probably had point given our audience. Honestly, breakfast sounded great but still.

"We can get some breakfast together very quickly." Marcella sounded like a mom. "Let's go and we can strategize the day because there will be a lot of questions, and we need to be ready."

SEVENTEEN

After a rejuvenating breakfast, Sofia took Eddie to the studio and that gave me time to work. Luckily, Eddie didn't make a fuss about going. Sofia enticed him by promising to also introduce him to a couple other artists who were recording that day as well.

Dad and Raptor, the director of TOS, had a lengthy discussion about the morning's events, and Raptor immediately deployed people to the scene. I'd also updated Lorenzo, and we identified more agents who should be able to help with the audio mystery.

Once we were off our calls, Mom, Dad, and I gathered around the small dining room table in their apartment.

"Did you feel anything at all before you got hostile?" Dad asked.

Mom looked up from her laptop, watching me, waiting. I was surprised he hadn't asked before, but it was good he'd waited because I was still processing the whole experience. At least the memories were filling in more.

"It's still hard to explain. As soon as I heard the music, it was like it scratched at my brain. You know how a scab itches or how annoying it feels when your arm's asleep and tingly? That's the best I can describe it. But it doesn't quite do the feeling justice either. The more I heard other noise, the worse it got. Every sound attacked me. If I hadn't gotten out of there, I don't know what I would've done. I wanted to attack John." I paused and suddenly couldn't face them, so I looked at the keyboard in front of me. "I knew it was all wrong, but I couldn't stop. I had to fight myself to leave because I really wanted to go back and beat up someone, anyone."

"That explains why there are so many injuries." Mom spun her laptop around, and I looked up to see pictures of the scene. "There were best friends who turned on each other. Others were attacked by strangers. From what we know, the tone affected 20 percent of the people, and it cut across all age groups, men and women. We don't know yet why it's that 20 percent and not more or less. When the music stopped, people calmed down quickly and reported that they felt weak—just like you."

"Are there any similar characteristics of the people who were impacted by the sound?" Dad asked.

"I've got a team looking for the similarities. I've also sent information about our group and how it only affected Theo." Her laptop beeped, and she asked for a moment. "We've got our first casualty," she finally continued. "Seventeen-year-old male had a brain hemorrhage and died at the hospital. It's unclear if it was caused due to injuries from the melee or the audio itself."

"The audio itself?" I asked. That didn't make sense.

"There's a note in the initial examination that reports auditory distress. They're working to determine actual cause of death."

TOS was doing its best to keep a lid on the cause of the violence while we did our work. We had a lot of the cell phone footage and were working behind the scenes to make sure what was out there didn't have the dangerous audio. How much the story could be controlled was a wild card, so we needed to hurry up and figure this out. Meanwhile, there were random reports of fights breaking out as people saw news reports.

The doorbell rang, and I had a pretty good idea what had just arrived.

"I'll get it."

Through the glass, I saw a woman holding a midsize box. Lorenzo, as usual, acted very quickly to get what I needed. We traded the code words to prove I was the recipient.

"What'd you get?" Dad asked as I returned to the table and tore into the box.

"Phones. I wanted a few to see if there was any change based on the device that was used."

So far this morning, the TOS team had focused on the violence but the other threat in the songs remained—stealing data off the devices that played them.

I called Lorenzo, and as soon as we properly identified, I put him on speaker. "Is there any evidence that people's electronic devices were compromised this morning?"

"Not that we know of," Lorenzo said. "We're on site analyzing the phones we have. It seems almost impossible that a device that's not already configured to do so could be triggered to send data due to an audio signal. But nothing about this case adds up. The assumption has been that data could only be stolen if the song was on the device, but we are checking."

"I'll experiment with the phones you sent as well. Any other news?"

"Not yet. Just a lot of analysis. Split Screen reports progress, though, on the data trace. It's insane how much they're hopping the data, parking it for a time and moving it again. We'll keep you posted on that. The expanded audio team is also getting to work."

"Thanks, Doc. Talk soon."

Something had changed in the audio component. I didn't freak out yesterday, even though the security was tripped. I still had that song on my laptop, and it was the best place to start an analysis.

"Do either of you have voice recognition activated on your computer or phones?" I looked to Mom and Dad. "If you do, I'm about to run a test that should yield a security alert."

"I don't have it active on my laptop, but it's on the phone," Dad said.

"I leave it off on all my devices unless I know I need it."

The answers didn't surprise me. Mom was more skittish about devices that listened all the time—far more than Dad was. He used Siri on his phone often.

I hit Play on my computer and the song started.

The laptop warning screen came up in a couple of seconds, followed almost immediately by my phone. Dad's went off next.

The alerts were so loud.

I slammed the laptop shut. The music didn't stop.

"Theo?" Dad asked.

I knocked the computer to the floor.

My head was about to explode.

"Make it stop!"

Mom stood and put her hands on my shoulders. I tried to stand and push her away, but she held me down.

"Victor!"

So much chaos.

"Try to stay calm." Mom's voice did nothing to soothe me.

"Don't tell me what to do."

I shoved the table, forcing it away and knocking over the chair Dad had been in. Mom still held firm.

What was I doing?

I reached for her hand, but she moved fast to get both my arms just above the elbow.

She forced my arms behind me.

"I don't know his password," Dad yelled.

It hurt. I had no leverage to get free.

"Get away from that!"

These were my parents. I shouldn't yell at them.

Thrashing around only made Mom increase her force.

Dad got earbuds from his messenger bag and jammed them into the laptop. The music faded to barely audible. It stopped as Dad used the inline earphone controller to stop the playback.

The brain itch stopped.

I slumped to the side, and Mom shifted to a lighter hold.

"It's okay," Mom said. "I've got you."

"I don't understand. Nothing happened when I played that yesterday. The security alerts went off and that was it. That was worse than hearing it on the TV."

Dad shot a concerned look at me and then at Mom.

"How's that possible?" Mom asked. "How has the file changed just sitting on your laptop."

She was right. It didn't make sense. No one had access to my laptop to plant a new file. I could see from the file info it was the same one. I accessed the internet through the Glenwood corporate network yesterday. Did that make a difference? It's the only thing I could think of that was different than yesterday.

Was that it? Could the file be manipulated through the internet? I was on our Wi-Fi hotspot. But what would be gained by activating the song to provoke violence only if the device was online?

"And you guys heard nothing out of the ordinary? Felt nothing?" They shook their heads.

"We heard the song and the alerts," Mom said.

"I want to do another test. I need those noise-canceling headphones. It's fascinating...." I paused to think. "While memory wasn't an issue, focus and concentration proved difficult. The desire to lash out happens so fast. Once it's over, though—" I made a whooshing sound. "—I'm spent."

Dad got the headphones from the couch where I'd laid them when we came in.

"Are you sure you're up for this now?" Mom asked. "You can just tell Lorenzo what to do." Even while she spoke, I retrieved the laptop to set up the experiment.

"There's no guarantee the conditions will be the same. It's a fairly safe bet that if I start that song over, the same thing will happen. The headphones will block it."

I turned on the noise-canceling function and slipped on the headphones.

"Can you guys say something?"

I barely heard myself. Mom and Dad's mouths moved, but I heard nothing.

"I'm gonna start the song over. If I start to freak at all, stop it. I'll try not to throw things this time." I smirked because the mood needed to be lightened. They gave a thumbs-up.

My finger hovered over the Play key, but I was hesitant to push it. The headphones seemed safe, but I was unsure. I bought a few moments while I opened up some analysis programs.

When I had everything set, I took a deep breath and pushed Play. The output meters showed music was playing but, thankfully, I heard and felt nothing. Dad stood by, though, ready to stop the playback.

Using the audio analyzer that I had added to my tools after Danny had demonstrated it yesterday, I compared the snapshot from yesterday and saw that the music was the same. However, the flat line was now larger. I let the song play to completion, so I'd have a complete look at it.

After the song played out, it was time to test a theory. Was it changed if the device was on the internet?

I took the laptop offline, reset the analyzer and pushed Play again. The audio pattern looked exactly like it did yesterday.

"I think I've figured it out, but I need to know for sure." I hoped I'd found the answer so I didn't have to feel the rage all over again. "Take the laptop. I'm removing the headphones. Be ready to stop the music."

Once Dad had the laptop, I raised my hands and removed the headphones slowly.

I heard the song.

There was no effect.

"You okay?" Mom asked, watching closely.

I nodded and set the headphones on the table. "So far." I gave it a minute just to make sure. "Totally normal. Start it over, please."

The start of the song had triggered me the last time. It was possible that whatever made me lose it was only in the beginning of the track. Dad did as I asked, and I was okay.

"This is weird, but it appears the file receives instructions from the internet."

"That's unbelievable. And scary." Mom sat down.

I nodded. "I'll update Lorenzo. We have to figure out where that signal's coming from and stop it."

EIGHTEEN

ONCE I'D FIGURED out the audio file got instructions from the internet, I spent the rest of the day on video conferences. A few brave souls at TOS HQ volunteered to be tested to see if the file affected them.

We also recovered the file from Atlanta, and it matched the one I had from the MDS. Since radio stations have different needs, they don't use the preview websites. In this case, the event's DJ transferred the song to the device the day before, so it was ready to go. That meant, however, the song didn't get updated. Making matters worse, the device was online so there was no stopping the violence-inducing signal.

We also confirmed the playback device had its data transmitted. Luckily it wasn't a personal phone, so all that was stolen were a few phone numbers. The code circumvented all of the antivirus protections. The phone had solid, consumer security in place, and it didn't protect the phone at all. Lorenzo activated another team to look at that, so we could help antivirus companies issue patches.

There were more reports of violence as well, which

were tied to people hearing the song as the reports about Atlanta aired on TV and cell phone video went up on social media. TOS and other agencies continued to scrub the song audio anywhere it cropped up. Doing that under the guise of the ongoing investigation got trickier, though. Any sign of a cover-up would only make controlling the story worse.

"I've never seen anything like this," Lorenzo said. "Not outside of the movies anyway. Any luck tracing what activates the audio signal?"

After several hours my team had nothing concrete. The code behind this was a very clever design. "So far, traces and blocks have failed."

"We've replicated the effects. The common factor is that it impacts people who can perceive sound at a particular low-level frequency, and it's devastating if they're exposed to it for more than a couple seconds. The longer they hear it, the more agitated they become."

"I don't think I'd heard it for more than thirty seconds at a time, and it was awful."

"They don't hear it so much as feel it," Lorenzo continued. "While only eighteen people were affected in Atlanta, once the fight broke out, it didn't really matter who had been affected and who hadn't. Crowd mentality took over and, except for the few people who got out of there right away, almost everyone ended up fighting."

"Anyone reporting memory issues after being exposed to it?"

"I was just about to bring that up. You and everyone in Atlanta reported memory issues in the immediate aftermath. But in the tests we've run since then, memory is intact. Subjects are just exhausted."

"Same for me. Doesn't seem like that's a fluke. So not only is it controlled through the internet, its effects can be modified. Can you imagine if the signal went out at a major event? The Super Bowl or something else?"

"I can't— Sorry, one moment." He didn't put me on hold for long. "Stand by while I patch us into a call with Defender, Snowbird, Red Hat, and Raptor."

I shuddered at what could've happened that had Raptor on the call with us. As head of TOS, his presence was not standard protocol.

"I'll get right to it," Raptor said once Lorenzo connected us. "Blackbird is behind what's happening with Glenwood Music. Twenty-five minutes ago, we heard from an agent we've had embedded with Blackbird for the past year. Overture stumbled on the information in discussion with other Blackbird operatives."

Blackbird. We'd done damage to their organization in Denver last fall, but apparently not enough. I knew from briefings I received that TOS constantly monitored Blackbird for potential threats. Of course, some of that was above my clearance level, such as knowing we had someone embedded with them.

"Overture verified what we've already pieced together about the two actions the files carry out. His message was interrupted before he could tell us more, and we don't know his present condition. We're taking the steps to get in touch with him. His chip indicates he's in Riverhead, New York. This situation is different from what he was involved with, which related to disrupting the World Bank. It's not clear if there's a connection."

And there it was—the culprit revealed. We still had to figure out how to stop them before a mass number of songs were released, either from Glenwood or some other source.

"There are indications this has been in the works for a few months. I had Telegraph look into a few things in our code repository," Red Hat said. "Winger, remember those strange alerts you got on your phone earlier this year, and we never could figure out what those were."

Those started around the time of the computer science competition—some incidents when Eddie was around and others that were random. It'd happened nine times over five weeks. I always logged the data into the TOS database for analysis, but the findings were always inconclusive.

"Yeah, of course."

"There's a similarity in the carrier waves. Perhaps those earlier incidents were tests. Plus we found it in other log reports from phones around the world. Taken separately it seems random and nothing ties them together individually, but now the connections are plain."

"What I don't understand is the tie between these signals and the kidnapping threats against the Glenwood's that brought us here in the first place." Dad voiced the question I'd already wondered about.

"We hoped you might have figured that out," Raptor said. "We agree it's not clear. They obviously wanted access to the distribution system, but that had to have been in progress before you arrived."

"Maybe the attempted abductions were just a smoke-screen." Mom offered her opinion.

"Perhaps," Raptor continued. "Defender and Snowbird, you reported that the Glenwoods would shut down their distribution system. Has that happened?"

"Yes," Mom said. "It went into maintenance mode within an hour after the Atlanta news broke. They also put on hold the company's releases for this week. The only channel that's left open is the streaming service they control and their team has made sure no infected tracks are present.

Access to that system is currently restricted to only Oliver Glenwood."

"Winger," Lorenzo chimed in, "can you verify that the security is good enough they shouldn't be able to be infiltrated from the outside."

"That's correct. My attacks from outside were repeatedly shut down. Like anything, if you work long enough, you'll probably find a way in, but they are buttoned up tight."

"Okay," Raptor said. "I'd like reports at least every four hours and more if you think it's worthy. The most important objective is finding where the signals causing the violence come from and shut it down."

"Understood." We all acknowledged.

"Thank you all. Raptor signing off."

"Winger, I need to update some teams," Lorenzo said. "I'll be back in touch with you later. Doctor Possible out."

"Snowbird and Defender, I'll see you when you're back at base. Winger out."

I disconnected and joined a call with Split Screen and the others working on tracing the incoming and outgoing signals from the song files.

NINETEEN

THE TEAM and I worked through the afternoon trying to figure out how to break down the files. We had to uncover how instructions were received.

Another team worked to trace the theft of the personal data from devices. We had the devices mimicking different areas of the country so our activity wouldn't be obvious. Blackbird, however, knew exactly what it was doing when it designed the program, making it almost impossible to track its actual source.

The situation bounced between maddening and fascinating. To assemble something like this and be able to bury it in the way Blackbird had showed extraordinary skill.

I was rarely so frustrated with myself as I'd been in the last few hours. Even when I can't accomplish the goal, I usually have an idea of where to start. Nothing I did moved us closer to an effective way to stop this. Yes, my colleagues had the same problem and that only made it worse because *none* of us had progress to report.

As I ran my analysis programs, with what felt like the

thousandth modification, my phone buzzed and a text from Eddie displayed.

Coming back from the studio with Sofia. She's picking up some dinner. Can I bring us some too?

I looked at the clock in the upper-right corner of the monitor. It was nearly seven. Despite the windows in front of me, I hadn't paid attention to how far the sun had moved across the sky, now casting long shadows.

I could afford a few minutes with Eddie to have dinner.

I texted back: *That'd be awesome. I could use some us time.*

The response came quickly: *Cool. See you soon.*

Perfect timing. My stomach rumbled right after I read his messages. A reminder I hadn't eaten since Christian brought lunch hours ago.

My phone lit up again, this time with an incoming call from Lorenzo.

"Winger, Doctor Possible here. Ghostlight is also here." Ghostlight was new to the team, and I hadn't met her in person because she worked in Seattle. Her specialties were far-reaching, and she already had a good reputation. She was part of the team tracing where the stolen data was going.

"Well, I hope one of you has good news because I feel like I'm banging my head against a brick wall."

"We may have some progress." Lorenzo actually sounded upbeat. "Ghostlight, do you want to go over what you just showed me?"

"Absolutely." She sounded eager, which I liked since it helped knock out some of my frustration. "Winger, I sent data to your screen."

The hazard of not bringing more than one laptop was that I had only the single screen. It was annoying in moments like when I wanted to display multiple things simultaneously.

"Got it. Go ahead."

"We've finally placed a tracker in a credit card data file so that the routine sending the data won't ignore it. However, we eventually lose the trace because it seems to go behind a firewall."

She'd made amazing progress even though she'd run into a new issue.

"That's great work. Nesting tracking into a file as small as credit card data is impressive. How can I help?"

"Doctor Possible tells me you are unparalleled in creating tracking bots. I'm curious about two things. If I give you what we sent out, can you find it? And can you review the tracking payload and find a better way for us to follow it."

I studied the information she shared. Improvements for the program flooded my mind.

"I can certainly try. I think the bot to find the data will be slightly easier, so I'll tackle that first. Doc, I'd also like to involve Amp. I think he'd be good at improving the payload."

"We can reassign him. I'll let him know and have him contact you two."

"I'll get to work on this and keep you both posted, especially when there's something to test."

"Fantastic," Ghostlight said. "Doc, I'll switch over to the team blocking the signal that interacts with the audio."

"That'd be great," Lorenzo said. "We've got to get that blocked. We've got spot reports of violence around the world. In some cases we can't be sure they're all related to this, but we've verified some are. It seems there are more songs out there than we might have realized."

I sighed, and I suddenly hated the chair I was sitting in. I'd spin around at home. That helped me think sometimes.

"I look forward to hearing progress soon. Doctor Possible out."

"Ghostlight out."

My screen returned to displaying my work. It was only a moment, though, before an email arrived from Ghostlight with the details I needed. I started going over the information and soon lost myself in it.

The knock at the door was perfectly timed—Eddie was often good at that. Dinner would let me formulate the plan for the tracking bot. I closed the computer and went to the door. Eddie smiled through the glass and held up a huge shopping bag.

"It's good to see you," I wrapped him in a hug. "Come on in."

"Sofia says I've brought the very best burgers in the city. They certainly smelled good in the car. I think we're in for a great dinner."

"Awesome." My mouth watered. I resisted snatching the bag from his hand because the burgers smelled incredible. "I didn't realize how hungry I'd gotten until you texted. My stomach's been loud ever since."

"Then let's eat." He grinned as if nothing else in our world mattered. I liked the temporary respite from the crazy.

He went to the dining room table and laid out the haul. I moved my laptop and notebook to the coffee table. I pocketed the phone just in case anyone buzzed.

"How much food did you get? There's only two of us, you know." I surveyed the five large containers on the table.

"Well, burgers and fries, of course. Onion rings too because Sofia says they're the best ever. There's dessert because they had this peanut butter cake, and I know you can't resist peanut butter. I only got one slice because it's ginormous." He held up a container bigger than the wrapped burger.

"You know I've got more work tonight, right? How am I going to avoid a food coma?"

He raised an eyebrow over the rim of his glasses. "I've seen you down massive amounts of food and act like it was nothing. I'm sure you'll be fine." He capped that remark with a super cute smirk.

"You might know me too well."

"Maybe." He folded the shopping bag and looked around the table. "I knew I forgot something. Drinks."

"No problem. There's plenty in the kitchen."

He retrieved two cans from the fridge. Unfortunately, there was no Dr Pepper as I'd drank all of those earlier and hadn't refreshed the supply from the main house. Pepsi would suffice.

Eddie put the drinks down, and we tore into the food. I couldn't believe how awesome it looked. He got me a bacon, pepper jack burger—my favorite. Neither of us spoke, unless you count the grunts the tasty food caused. Sofia was right about these. Whatever they spiced the burger meat with was incredible and that spice blended so perfectly with the cheese.

"It was really cool hanging out with Sofia today," Eddie said once conversation could start again. "I had no idea how similar you two would be."

"How so?"

"You both get into an intense zone. She spent most of the afternoon working on an arrangement with one of her cowriters. The basics of the song were always there, but they'd manipulate it with different instruments in the forefront or changing the key. It drastically changed the feel of the song. Anyway, she was so focused, it was like nothing existed outside of the studio. I've seen you with that laser focus too."

While we'd devoured the burgers fairly quickly, we took our time savoring the fries and rings.

"Have you been able to figure out the stuff from this morning?" he asked, shifting the discussion. I don't know why I thought he'd stay away from it, even though I hoped he would. "I know you can't say too much, but since I saw some of the scary stuff, I thought I could at least ask."

"Yeah, this morning was... awful." He reached out and took my hand in his. "It's been a long afternoon, but there's been progress."

"Are you holding up okay?"

"Mostly. I can't believe I went off like that. At least I feel normal again."

"How much work do you have? Any chance we get to chill for a while?"

It was nice he opened with *how much* instead of *do you have to*. "I'm not sure yet. Dinner with you has helped me think through some aspects of what I need to create. I need to see if any of it's viable. You can watch TV, while I work here. Once I'm done... maybe you don't have to go upstairs tonight."

"You know just what to say." He held my gaze. "This feels so much like what we could have once we get our own place."

"Right? Except I doubt it would be this nice."

"What do you mean? You've saved up. You can't put us up in style?"

Oh my God. I loved his playfulness. It counteracted my difficult day, lifting a weight off me for at least a few minutes. I leaned over and kissed him. The salt from the fries and rings on our lips made the taste even better than usual.

"I love you."

I pulled back just enough to look at him. We stayed still, holding our gaze, until he kissed me again.

"We should move on to dessert." He stayed with his forehead against mine. "That way you can get back to work so we can get on to what comes after sooner."

I gave him one more quick kiss before he stood and brought the dessert container closer. What he revealed was probably the most decadent thing I'd ever seen. It looked like a tall, blonde brownie covered in chocolate and peanut butter sauce. Despite how much food I'd already put away, I wanted that bad.

"They told me to pop this in the microwave for a few seconds. Be right back."

"Can you bring another soda too?"

"Can do."

I watched him as he got the brownie warming and got the drinks. I swear the more he swam the more gracefully he moved. He was doing normal things, but I couldn't take my eyes off him. Just as the microwave beeped he threw a wink my direction. Such a goofball. He managed to bring the dessert, sodas, and forks to the table in one trip.

"Best-looking waiter ever," I said.

"Don't forget, you can tip me later."

I looked forward to doing just that.

The dessert was too much. We only made it through about half. I couldn't remember the last time I'd been this full. Maybe Thanksgiving.

"I suppose that could become breakfast." I looked between what was left on the plate and Eddie.

"Or late-night snack. We may need the energy."

"Someone's extra horny."

"Maybe. You've been gone a few days."

"You made it while I was gone for that internship. That was a couple of weeks."

He stood and offered a hand to me, which I used to pull myself up.

"Yeah, but I knew that was coming. I'd barely had any time with you before you came down here."

I stole some kisses. This time he tasted of peanut butter and that was yummy. I sucked on his bottom lip.

"Let me get to work," I finally said. "The sooner I finish, the sooner it can be just us."

Of course, we ended up making out for a few minutes, wrapping ourselves around each other as best we could as we stood near the small table we'd eaten at.

"Okay, okay." I forced myself back. "If we don't stop, I'm not gonna get anything done. Go sit and find yourself something to watch. I'll work as fast as I can."

He sighed. "You're evil." He pressed my hand against the bulge in his shorts. "You did this and now you want me to watch TV?"

I gave his hardness a quick squeeze before I stepped back. "I have no doubt you'll be able to get that back." I spun him around and gave him a gentle shove toward the couch. I nudged him along since I needed to get my laptop. As we moved he provided just enough resistance to keep it fun.

"You could just sit on the couch with me."

"You know I wouldn't be able to focus if I did. It'll be hard enough with you so close."

God, he looked so good. I hoped the ideas I'd conceived

during dinner were something I could execute fast. I really didn't want to do anything but get us naked.

I situated myself at the table with my soda. Every time I looked up from my screen, I saw the back of Eddie's head and the TV as he clicked through channels.

It turned out, my brain worked hard during dinner. Within half an hour, I'd sent over a few different versions of a bot to better track the data Ghostlight had tagged. I recommended deploying all of them because the more tracers we had in the field, the better chance we had for at least one of them to find it.

Eddie watched *Lip Sync Battle*, one of his favorite programs. I found the show amusing with how far celebrities would go to win.

As I moved to my other task, I alternated between being amused by Eddie's commentary—he had a lot to say about song choices—and coding. The TV sound was welcome after wearing headphones so much today. I hadn't realized how much noise there usually was around me, and it'd been weird to work in such complete silence.

Suddenly I went limp. My head crashed down on the keyboard.

What the hell?

I couldn't lift myself.

I couldn't form words. Even mumbles were difficult.

I could see, but it was fuzzy.

The computer screeched because I laid on the keys.

Why wasn't Eddie doing something? He had to hear the noise. The TV wasn't that loud.

He finally came over but moved slowly like he wanted to creep up on me. I couldn't see his face because I couldn't move my head to look up.

He sat me up and angled my head so I could see his face.

"I'm sorry, Theo."

Sorry? For what? Why was he so calm?

I tried to struggle... to move... anything. Nothing responded.

He gently let my head drop until my chin was on my chest. He wrapped his arms around me and the chair so he could slide it back.

I had to move.

The comm was muted for outgoing so no one would hear. Currently the earpiece only recorded for the contacts.

Shit. My computer was open and unlocked. I had to get to it.

I focused on moving but couldn't.

My breathing increased with the struggle. What was I going to do?

Why wasn't Eddie getting my parents?

His hands were suddenly under my legs and behind my back. He scooped me out of the chair.

This would've been romantic under different circumstances.

Where were we going?

Panic gripped me. My lungs worked overtime as my muscles refused to execute the instruction my brain sent.

"You need to calm down."

He gently laid me on the bed and arranged me—legs straight, arms at my side, head on a pillow. All I could see was the ceiling.

Was he?

No way. I'd have known. Someone would've known.

Eddie leaned over, and I could see him. "I really do love

you. I've got no choice in this." His voice cracked. Was he crying? "I know you won't believe that. But it's true."

He leaned over and kissed my forehead before walking away. There was noise, but I couldn't figure out what it was, other than the TV.

Nothing worked. My body had been turned off. I could breathe and see. My heart beat.

Would those fail too?

What did he mean no choice?

A few moments later the door opened and closed.

Tears fell, and I couldn't wipe them away.

TWENTY

WHY WAS I SHAKING? And who was talking?

I struggled to open my eyes, but it was difficult. Crap. The contact lenses were still in.

Voices became clearer. Mom, Dad, maybe John too. All at once.

"I think we need 911," Dad said.

"No," I croaked out. Hopefully they heard.

"Theo?"

Mom seemed close to panicked. She never sounded that way. I still couldn't open my eyes.

What happened? I'd been working.

"Where?"

No, that's not what I needed to ask. We were in New York.

"Eye drops."

"Eye drops?" Dad asked.

"Yes." Every word was so difficult. I couldn't remember feeling this bad—ever.

"Try the bathroom."

The eye drops weren't there.

"Back," I mumbled. "Backpack."

"Theo." Mom sounded calmer. "Why the eye drops?"

"Contacts...."

But why? Why would I sleep in them?

When did I get in bed?

And where was Eddie? He watched TV and I worked. The TV was on, playing some commercial.

"I'm sorry, Theo."

And it all crashed back.

"No. No. No." I think I shook my head, but I wasn't sure.

"Theo? What?" Mom again.

"What's happened?" Now Dad.

My chest clinched tight—so much anger and sadness raged in my soul. The physical pain or the reactions to fear I'd experienced in the past months as an agent had nothing on the fire that burned through me. The strength of the emotion nearly overwhelmed the physical issues I experienced in the aftermath of whatever Eddie had given me.

"Got 'em." I recognized John now.

"We got the eye drops." Mom used her mom voice. "I'm going to wet your eyes. A little bit at a time. Okay?"

"Yeah."

The liquid felt good as it seeped past my eyelashes. I moved my eyeballs around to get everything wet. Finally I opened my eyes. Mom, Dad, and John stood close to the bed with Oliver keeping a distance. I blinked to get my eyes to focus while I struggled to sit up against the headboard.

"We need to talk." I looked between Mom and Dad, and they nodded.

"Oliver, we need a few minutes." Mom frowned and furrowed her brow.

"You want me here or with the family?" John asked.

"Since we don't know what's happened, you should probably stick with the Glenwoods." Mom's tone was crisp, more professional than usual. She'd recovered from her panic. "We'll keep you posted."

I wanted John here, though. We considered him family. But we had to be agents, and the mission was seriously compromised.

John nodded. It was easy to see he didn't like being sent away, but he and Oliver left without another word.

Dad pulled out his phone and tapped on the screen. "I opened my comm channel so John can hear."

"Theo," Mom said, the concern coming right back to her voice, "what's happened?"

I opened my mouth to talk but all that happened was that my breathing increased. Mom ran her hand through my hair. Even that couldn't penetrate the powerful wave of emotions.

"I've been compromised." My body shook, and I didn't know if it was emotional, physical, or both. "Lorenzo needs to fry my electronics ASAP. All of them. The stuff at home too." The words vibrated, making it sound like I was chattering from the cold.

I took a deep breath and looked between them. Their shocked looks plunged another emotional knife through me.

My next words would only make it worse.

"Eddie drugged me." A weird whimper came out at the end of the sentence. I'd never made a sound like that before. Sobs threatened to spill out, and I worked hard to keep them locked inside. "I don't know how." I struggled to breathe deep to find some calm before I flew apart. "He paralyzed me. My computer was open."

I closed my eyes as my throat threatened to give over to

the outburst that wanted out. "I have no idea what he may have seen."

Mom and Dad traded horrified looks. Mom's look softened and she put her hand on my forearm, squeezing gently. She was still being a mom even as she faced an agent who'd completely fucked everything up.

"I'll get Lorenzo on it." Dad sounded like he was holding anger back—I didn't know if it was aimed at me or the situation. "We'll get someone here to draw blood and figure out what's in your system. Especially if there'll be any aftereffects." He tapped on his phone. "We'll figure this out. I know this isn't easy." He leaned over and put his hand on top of Mom's, squeezing both of us. "First and foremost we're your parents, and you come first."

"I know." The shake in my voice was embarrassing. An agent doesn't behave like this. "I know. Please call Lorenzo. He needs to take out those electronics."

Dad nodded.

I'd have to deal with the ramifications of losing a boyfriend later. More important things were at stake.

"Dr. Possible, Defender here. We have a code black situation. All of Winger's access needs to be revoked and his electronics destroyed immediately."

He was silent for a moment and then finished with only a "thanks." He dropped the phone into his pants pocket. "He's on it. He'll call back as soon as it's done."

"What happened?" Mom asked.

I related the story of dinner and what came after. I barely found the strength to get through it using the calming techniques I'd learned from Shields. Eddie had cut me at every level. I don't think I could've done the same to him if I'd been ordered to. I love... loved him. He'd shattered everything I'd believed about us.

The more I talked, the easier it became. My body started to loosen up too, and I was able to move better.

"I don't know what to say." Dad's face was creased, looking more worried than I'd ever seen. "How could we miss that as careful as we are?"

We were constantly aware of the people that we got close to. Everyone who set foot in our house had deep background checks run. They were submitted to the agency for review—preferably before they arrived. That included Eddie and his parents, Mitch and Iris, my teammates and classmates and all their parents. So many people were vetted to make sure that if there was anybody suspicious, we would at least know where we needed to safeguard.

Then there was my own security breach last night. I trusted Eddie too much. There'd never been another time where I had worked on classified code when anyone else, had been in the room. Last night it seemed secure enough since he wasn't standing over my shoulder.

Is there anyone else I should worry about? Are Mitch and Iris who I think they are? They are my closest friends besides Eddie—but are they really? Has someone flipped them against me?

Mom and Dad looked at me. Had I missed a question? Were they waiting for me?

"What do we do now?" I asked, voice soft. fearing the question. TOS would likely strip me of my clearances and fire me. Do agents get fired? Or does something worse happen?

"For now, we keep going," Dad said. "There's a mission to finish, and you're still part of the team. We will get you checked out physically to make sure you're okay. There will certainly be debriefings." He didn't sound happy about that last part.

Mom nodded and continued. "And we'll take care of our son. This is more than a mission setback. I can't imagine how you feel."

She was so earnest that it was hard for me not to crack. My first love smashed my heart. At some point my feelings about that would come out, but right now the agent part of me was too angry.

But seriously, how could someone be so cute and perfect over dinner and then pull that. This was real life, not a 007 movie.

Honestly, I'm not sure I can even tell if I'm angry or devastated. Winger needed to be in more control than Theo —I was sure of that.

Dad's phone rang and it snapped me back from being in my head. "Yes, Doc," he said. "He's seems okay. I can put you on speaker. Actually, let me run a quick bug check. Stand by."

We'd checked for bugs when we'd arrived, but this recheck was valid given the circumstances. He walked around the apartment and after a couple minutes he was back at the bed.

"We're all clear. Putting you on speaker, Doc."

"Snowbird here."

They looked at me. How could I say the words given how I'd messed up? "Winger—" Anxiety welled up again, trying to cut off my speech. "Winger here." Turned out to be the hardest words I'd said all morning.

I adjusted to sit cross-legged on the bed.

"Winger, good to hear from you. I wasn't sure what to expect after the code black." Lorenzo's concerned voice stabbed my heart. At least he kept any anger or disappointment at bay. "Tell me what happened."

"Have you shut down all the access?"

That had to be the first thing. We had to ensure what Eddie stole couldn't be used by anyone.

"We've taken out everything. The laptop you had with you plus the computers you had on at home have been rendered useless. The ones that were offline will be fried the next time they come online. Everything is backed up in the cloud, of course, so we can restore and restart your access under new credentials when you're ready."

Would they really just reactivate my access? I wasn't sure if I trusted myself.

"What's the story?" Lorenzo pressed the question.

I recounted the tale again. The memories were clearer this time, so I filled in even more details.

"We'll see how far we can track Eddie. Your phone should've tracked him until we zapped it. As far as we can tell he didn't try to access it because the security didn't engage. It doesn't look like he tried to use the laptop either. The logs show it was in standby mode from about ten forty last night until we sent the wipe signal. And we got the response from the phone, laptop, and most of your home equipment confirming they were zapped."

"You said the computer was in standby?"

"Unless something was done to send us false information, yes," Lorenzo said.

Would Eddie have closed the laptop? If he did, maybe he hadn't seen much, unless he read what was on the screen. After he'd put me on the bed, it was only a couple of minutes before he left.

"I had the contacts in last night. You should have data up to the point the phone went out of range. Maybe we can see when he slipped me whatever drug he used. And what happened afterward."

"I'll get that pulled from the cloud. I'll handle the

analysis on that myself." I heard him type. I'd thank him later for doing the review instead of someone else seeing the disaster play out.

"And you've got all my code from last night?"

"We haven't looked in depth yet, but it would seem so from what I see on my screen now. As the laptop went into standby, it transmitted the last bit of your work."

"Good. I'd just started on an idea to block the audio transmission."

"I'll get you new electronics immediately. You want them delivered to the same place as the test devices?"

How was there no reprimand? How could he trust me? I didn't really know what to say.

"Doc," Mom stepped in. "Send the equipment to the same address. We need to talk here, and we'll get back in touch with you."

"Understood, Snowbird."

Dad disconnected the call.

"Theo, what are you thinking?" Dad asked.

I unfolded my legs and very ungracefully got up. I still wore the shorts and T-shirt from yesterday, and I felt gross. I opened my mouth to speak, but where did I even start. I'd failed as an agent. I'd failed as a colleague. I'd failed as a boyfriend. I wasn't prepared to handle any of that.

Dad's phone buzzed. He looked and typed a reply.

"John's bringing some breakfast," Dad said. "He figured you could use it."

I wasn't sure I could eat, but I'd give it a try. What I needed for sure was water. Shuffling into the kitchen in my sock feet, I pulled a glass from the cupboard and filled it with tap water. I drank it down and filled it again. Mom and Dad followed and stared.

"Theo, we know this isn't easy," Dad continued. "It's

never easy being let down by someone you love. We'll listen to whatever you need to say."

I put the glass on the counter and moved quickly toward Dad. He knew what I needed because his arms were out. I crashed into him, wrapping my arms around his back. Mom hugged from behind, and I was nested between the two people who would always take care of me.

I quaked as they held tight. No tears came. Maybe everything was too mixed up. There were sobs—heavy ones. At least I felt safe.

We stayed like that for several minutes, which gave me time to collect my thoughts. I couldn't recall a time I'd been so unsure about the path forward. Usually there were clear signs even if I was hesitant.

We needed to find out how we all missed Eddie being an enemy. A passing comment Lorenzo made months ago after a couple of weird incidents involving Eddie came to mind: was someone using him to get to me? At the time we'd brushed it off. It was a couple of weird signals and an infected thumb drive that never added up. I'd reported it but never followed up. Had Lorenzo? If he had, he surely would've told me, or at least told my parents, to be on the lookout.

I had to focus on this case so no one else could be hurt by these music files. Time to get back to work.

I finally released my hold on Dad, and they both stepped back.

"What do you want to do?" Mom asked.

"Finish this mission. And then figure out what happened."

"We *all* missed the signs," she said. "I know this impacts you the most, but it's not all on you. Don't carry the weight on your own."

"I know."

Most of me believed that. But as much time as I spent with Eddie, I would've thought there'd been clues to what he was capable of. What did they say about me, though? I wasn't who I appeared to be either. His deceptions proved more successful than mine.

"I should call Lorenzo and debrief on what I was working on last night."

"Okay." Mom went to Dad, getting ready to go. "We'll let you get to it. Once you're done and get yourself put together, why don't you come up and work with us. We plan to be based here most of the day."

I nodded. It'd be nice to spend the day with them since it would help keep my mind off Eddie. "I'll be up in a few."

They each came in for another hug, and I returned them happily. I appreciated they weren't trying to sugarcoat anything but were simply there for me in any way I needed.

TWENTY-ONE

"We'll have a new laptop and phone to you within the next two hours. A courier departed by plane not too long ago," Lorenzo said. "I looked at what you have on the cloud from last night, and it looks like there's good stuff there. Hopefully you can—" He abruptly stopped, which was unusual. "Stand by, Winger. We're getting some new information."

I hated not having a computer in front of me because he could've shared with me immediately. It was already a breach of protocol to use Dad's phone without him present.

"Do you know if Glenwood Music turned the distribution system back on?" Lorenzo asked.

"It's supposed to stay in maintenance until we gave the all clear."

"It appears it's online or something else changed. We're seeing songs replaced with infected files at a rapid rate."

This was a disaster. There were thousands of songs in the Glenwood system and consumers could be receiving tainted music.

"Let me see what I can find out. You can reach me on

Defender's phone until mine arrives. And—" I sighed. This was so frustrating. "Never mind. I was going to get on comms, but I can't do that without authorized electronics. So, yeah, reach me on Defender's."

"Will do, Winger." He paused for a brief moment. "We'll get this sorted. I promise."

I appreciated Lorenzo. Even when we worked together he often talked more as my friend than an agent or my superior.

We said our goodbyes and disconnected. I abandoned the idea of getting cleaned up and went up to Mom and Dad's. The door was locked, so I knocked and as Mom came to the door, Oliver came down the stairs next door. He did not look happy. The news of the distribution system's activation must've reached him as well.

"I assume you've both heard the latest?" Mom said as she stood aside so Oliver and I could enter.

"I just got off the phone with IT," Oliver said as we went into the dining room where Dad was. "They have no idea how the system restarted, and they haven't been able to shut it down."

"How long has it been going?" I asked.

"A little over an hour, and it's distributed updates ever since. It started with the most current material, and it's going backward."

I looked between my parents, which I'd done so much this morning as I tried to recover from losing my heart. Mom stood next to me, arms crossed. Dad was seated at his computer. They didn't have the answers for this. I was still the IT guy in charge, so the call was mine. "We need to get to the office and try to shut this down. If we're lucky, we'll be able to trace who initiated this."

"Agreed," Mom and Dad said, nearly as one.

"Take John with you," Dad said. I handed over his phone. "And be careful."

"I'll call for the car and meet you outside in five minutes." Oliver was out the door like a shot.

"Can you call Lorenzo, please, and ask him to divert the courier to Oliver's office?"

"Of course." Mom was about to say more and stopped.

"What? Tell me."

"I was about to be 'Mom,' but I know you're trying to be professional."

"Thanks."

Outside, John, Oliver, and Sofia were already on the stairs waiting for the car. I asked them to give me a minute, and I hustled into my apartment. There was no time to shower, but I swapped out shirts and ran wet fingers through my hair. I grabbed my backpack and was outside just as the car pulled up.

"Sofia you take the front," John said. "I want to hang with Theo."

Sofia nodded. She must have some idea of how sideways the morning had gone. Her demeanor was very businesslike today, different from anything else I'd seen from her so far.

We all piled in the SUV, and John and I had the back seat to ourselves.

He reached into his backpack and handed me a wrapped, warm sandwich and a Dr Pepper. "One bacon and egg sandwich." He then dropped to a whisper. "You know I'm here if you want to talk."

I simply nodded. There was no doubt that I'd take him up on his offer later. I looked out the window, ignoring the food in my hands. Brooklyn raced by. I'd planned to make time, so Eddie and I could get out to explore.

I leaned my forehead against the window as the scenery sped by.

"I'm sorry, Theo." I pulled away from the window and found Sofia leaning around her seat. "I don't know what happened, and it's not my business. But I didn't mean to cause trouble between you and Eddie. I was just trying...."

"Thanks. But it wasn't your fault."

There was nothing more to say. Although, had it played into some grand master plan for Eddie to be here? Or was it coincidence? Had this been planned all along and this turned out to be a good time to execute. So many possibilities for me to overthink.

"If there is anything I can do, let me know," Sofia said. I nodded and when I didn't say more she turned back.

The rest of the ride went by in silence. I texted Lorenzo on John's phone to let him know I was headed to the office to work at the source. He had the team on standby for any support I required.

He also reported that Amp had taken the code I'd created as a payload tracker and worked with Ghostlight to integrate it.

The audio signal that causes the violence had gone dormant just after midnight last night. That couldn't be good. They were no doubt waiting to get the maximum amount of music in place before they turned it on again. We had to end this before that happened.

As soon as we pulled into the garage under the Glenwood building, Oliver got a call which he briefly took before turning to me. "Melissa's waiting for you in the office you used yesterday. Christian let her know that you needed a laptop, and it's ready to go."

"Thanks. I'll send out updates as I have them."

I went directly to the office, and there were three laptops along with a couple screens. It was perfect.

"They're all on the network." Melissa walked in behind me. "You can arrange them anyway you want. I figured more screens would be better." She'd pulled together very good setup in a short time "Is there anything I can do?"

I dropped my pack on the floor and a wave of anger passed through me as I realized I had nothing to get out of it. "Not right now." I kept my frustration to myself. "Thanks."

"I understand your intention is to shut down the distribution system completely."

"Yes, and at the same time trace who has control of it."

"We're completely locked out. Our ability to even take it off the network is hampered because of the built-in redundancies. Do you think you'll be able to?"

"I hope so."

I sat down and got to work. Someone had put an impressive wall set up around MDS in the last twelve hours or so. The traces I ran were manipulated inside the network. The question was by who and how.

"Can we terminate everyone's network access except for people who are accessing this system," I asked Melissa, who worked on the opposite side of the desk.

"But no one can get in," she said.

"Someone's in there, and if we terminate the login, it might break their lock on the system. There may also be people logged in that we can use to get access."

Her expression clouded. "This will cause a lot of chaos since most people will be blocked from legitimate work." She looked to me as if hoping I'd change my mind. "We should get Oliver's authorization." She went to use her phone.

"I've already got authorization to do whatever I think's necessary. And the fewer people who know the plan, the better."

She nodded slowly. "Okay, then." She came around the desk, and I gave her the chair, so she could do what was necessary.

I had no way to tell Dad the plan. In fact, if I thought about it too much, my lack of devices freaked me out. If I disrupted the network and found who this person was, we'd need to apprehend them and I had no way to tell anyone.

"Can I borrow your phone?" I asked.

"Um, sure." She unlocked it with her thumb before I took it.

I dialed John on his personal line.

"Hey, John. It's Theo. Can you come down? I need someone standing by."

"Sure. I'll be right there."

I passed the phone back.

"What about not sharing the plan?"

"John's with me, and not someone who's logged in from anywhere."

She sighed. Some people were uncomfortable not following processes, but sometimes you had to go outside the box.

On one of the screens, Melissa had the admin console displayed. Over a thousand logins were active—staff inside and outside this building. This console didn't show what systems people were logged in to by default, but based on my earlier review, I knew we could easily find out.

"What's the update?" John asked when he arrived, and I laid out the plan. We needed to be on alert so that when we figured out where the person who had control of the system was, they could be captured.

"How much time do you need to be ready?" John asked.

"I've already made it so people can't log in," Melissa said. "Once we log people out, they can't get back in. We can proceed when you're ready."

"We shouldn't delay," John said. "Here's a spare phone. We can use it to stay in touch. I'll stand by in Oliver's office so we can take action when you're ready. Your parents will be here within five for additional backup."

Where had he gotten a spare phone? Great that he had it, though. It wasn't secure, but it was better than nothing.

"That'll work," I said.

In a couple of minutes John buzzed, indicating he was back in position. Melissa had written the commands for the login system, so it would log people out unless they were in the distribution system. Everyone on the network had their own IP address assigned and that would be traceable to the computer they used, whether it was in the building or a remote connection.

In no time the login list had a single name besides the login Melissa used. Lawrence Bowman was a senior accountant logged in from his desk on the twelfth floor.

"We've got something." I pointed at the screen for Melissa to see. I called John and gave him the details.

"We're on it. I'm going with Glenwood security. We'll intercept, and as soon as we're locked down, I'll let you know."

"Understood. Standing by."

It was a tense few moments before the call came back. While we waited, Melissa managed a number of calls and emails about why no one could get on the network. She called it "emergency maintenance" and said her team was working on restoration. I appreciated her on-the-fly answer, which assured few questions.

The phone rang finally, and it was John. "We've appre-hended Mr. Bowman. You can shut the computer down."

"On it. Stand by."

We had the commands ready for the logout, but they didn't work. Despite repeated tries, we couldn't force the session to terminate.

"I can't get him off the network," Melissa said.

"I'm coming to you," I told John as I headed out of the office. "We can't break the connection remotely." I hung up and grabbed my pack.

"I'm coming with you." Melissa stood and I didn't try to discourage her.

We moved quickly through the halls, and I stopped at the stairs. We were on the sixteenth floor, and with only four floors to go down, that route seemed faster than waiting for the elevator. Melissa had no complaints.

On twelve we found people standing near the office that must be Lawrence's. We navigated our way through the crowd.

"I don't know what you're talking about," a man, no doubt Lawrence, said loudly. "All I'm doing is running the daily financial analysis reports. Of course, I'm logged in."

I walked in and sat down at his computer. John and two security guys covered him while Oliver stood by.

"What's he doing? Who is that? Mr. Glenwood, is he authorized to be in our financials?"

Bowman, for his part, seemed genuinely confused. I didn't wait for answers. I started the traces to find out why I couldn't break the network connection.

"He's more than authorized" was Oliver's only response.

It only took a moment for me to see that this terminal was hijacked. Hopefully the person in control didn't have eyes on this office because if we lost this lead it'd be a huge setback. Given the skill I'd seen, they had to be aware that something tried to boot them off the network.

"John, can you clear the room and give me your phone?" I turned toward John.

He simply nodded and traded me his unlocked TOS phone for the one he'd given me earlier. Oliver and his security men quietly followed but Lawrence continued to demand information.

Once John closed the door, I called Lorenzo.

"Doctor Possible, Winger here on Shotgun's phone."

"What've you got, Winger?"

I gave him the rundown. "Can you grant Shotgun's phone access to my cloud? I need some of my tools."

"Can do," Lorenzo said. "Stand by."

The time ticked by at an excruciating pace as the minutes stretched out. I waited and watched the monitor, hoping the intruder would stay put long enough for me to get access to what I needed.

"I've done one better, though, Shotgun may not be too happy. I've reconfigured his phone so it's yours now. When your new phone arrives, I'll switch it so it's his."

"You're awesome, Doc." I pulled a USB cable from my pack and plugged into the computer. "I've connected the phone so you can look at this too."

The code on the terminal was small and impressive. It bypassed all of Glenwood's security, allowing it to stay online. There was even a routine that kept the machine from fully powering down, so it stayed active and created a constant back door.

"While I figure out where this connection leads, can you pull an image of the drive so we can analyze this code more fully?" I asked Lorenzo.

"On it."

In a few minutes, I was able to lock on to the data packets that the malware sent and received. Heavily compressed data went in and out every few seconds. It would scarcely be detected as an increase in traffic. I quickly added what Ghostlight developed to the outgoing data, so we'd have the trace.

A knock at the door interrupted my analysis.

I didn't want just anyone coming in, so I went over and opened it a crack. Since it was John, I let him enter.

"We've been asked to go to Oliver's office. Apparently, all hell is breaking loose."

Dread washed over me. What was it now?

"We need someone stationed outside this door," I said. "Doc, plant a watch program on this computer so you can monitor. I've got to disconnect the phone."

His response was nearly instantaneous. "Done."

"How far out is the courier with my electronics?"

"Let me check." Lorenzo's keyboard clacking sounded. "Looks like ten minutes, maybe less, depending on traffic. I'll request the courier only put them in your hands or Shotgun's."

"Good. Lobby security should know where we are. As soon as I'm back with this computer, I'll call."

"Understood."

TWENTY-TWO

CHAOS REIGNED UPSTAIRS. Oliver's office was large, but it didn't feel that way as more than thirty people were packed into rows of chairs that had been laid out. At some point the couches and chairs and small conference table had been taken away to allow for this gathering.

There was a podium in front of Oliver's desk. I didn't see Oliver, though. Christian was up front, to the left of the podium. He looked sternly at the crowd as if daring anyone to do something that wasn't appropriate.

John had briefed me on the way up that Oliver was about to make a statement to the press. Mom and Dad, using their federal agency credentials, would make additional comments. John and I were to be bystanders at the back of the room with other Glenwood execs.

Oliver followed by Mom and Dad came into the room and went to the podium. Marcella and Sofia followed, but instead of going to the podium, they stood with me and John. The Glenwoods had never looked so stern, even in the face of the kidnappings. I imagined none of them liked what Oliver was about to say.

"Good morning, ladies and gentlemen, thank you for gathering at such short notice." Christian moved to stand behind the desk as Oliver spoke. "As you know, for the past few days the distribution systems of Glenwood Music have been offline. I can share with you today that they will remain so for the foreseeable future because we've been the victim of a cyberattack that has infected our song files with code dangerous for our customers. Despite our best efforts, music that's been previously purchased is vulnerable as well. As such, we encourage anyone with Glenwood Music songs on their devices to refrain from playing them and to delete them as soon as possible."

Oliver's pained expression upset me. He worked his entire life to build the company and this could be a fatal blow. And not just for him and his business but for the artists who recorded with him.

"We take these acts against the company very seriously and are cooperating with federal agencies to swiftly end this threat and restore safe music files to our customers. I'd like to turn this briefing over to Victor and Katherine Reese. Victor is with the Department of Homeland Security and Katherine with the FBI. They'll give brief remarks. We will not take questions as we do not want to compromise the investigation."

It was surreal seeing Mom and Dad in non-TOS roles. Occasionally they'd use these credentials to integrate with local officials more easily. To see them briefing the press was highly unusual but also kinda cool.

"Thank you, Oliver. I'm Victor Reese, a senior director for the Department of Homeland Security. We're investigating, along with the FBI and other agencies, the infiltration of Glenwood Music and its assets that have been compromised. As Oliver alluded to, the digital songs that have been distributed by the company pose a potential threat to consumers. We are doing everything we can to locate the parties responsible for the intrusion. As mentioned it is recommended that anyone who has songs from Glenwood Music delete them without further play. We've also asked radio and streaming services to suspend playing songs from online sources and delete any that are in the libraries. I'll now turn this over to my colleague from the FBI." Dad stepped aside for Mom.

"I am Special Agent Katherine Reese with the FBI Cyber Crime Division. We are actively looking for any details related to this breach of Glenwood Music and its systems. We are offering a reward of up to ten million dollars, which Mr. Glenwood is matching, for information that leads to the arrest and conviction of anyone who is involved in this serious crime, which includes a manslaughter charge as a result of the listening-party incident in Atlanta."

My phone buzzed, and the screen had a message from Lorenzo that we had a location. I nudged John and showed him the screen. He nodded, and I gestured at the door.

Back on the twelfth floor, people were back at their desks. Many watched the press conference and spoke in hushed tones. Lawrence Bowman was being kept in a nearby cubicle with two Glenwood security men blocking the door to his office. Melissa, meanwhile, worked at a cubicle just outside the office.

"I hope you've found something." She sounded stern. "I can't imagine the impact that press conference will have."

"I'm about to get some updates," I went to the office, and the two guards stepped aside.

"I'm afraid you'll need to stay out here." John blocked Melissa as she tried to follow.

"I've been with Theo for a couple of days now. What's changed?"

"He's been assigned directly to Homeland Security so any information he obtains has to go through the proper channels. I'm sure you understand."

She gave John an icy look but nodded. "I'll have to speak to Mr. Glenwood about this."

"Do what you need to do." John's tone shut down any further discussion. I had no idea the rules had changed, but John could easily have information I didn't.

Inside the office I immediately connected to Lorenzo, who patched me into a conference call. John stood at the door.

"Winger has joined the call," Lorenzo said. "As I was saying, within the last fifteen minutes, our traces have converged at a residential home just outside Philadelphia. Agents are in route while we attempt to extract as much information as we can from the servers there. We'll proceed cautiously so we don't trip any security features. As the press conference started, the audio signal that induces violence reactivated. We're trying to block that with a method Split Screen designed. Winger and Amp, I'd like you to work with them and see if you can add anything there."

"This is Ghostlight. We know the servers in Philly have heavy security measures, so it may take some time to extract all the data. We have high confidence. However, this is the final repository of the stolen data as there is no detectable outbound data from this location."

"Thank you, Ghostlight," Lorenzo said. "The work to retrieve the data, along with blocking the audio signal, are the top priorities. Ghostlight will coordinate with agents in Philadelphia to make sure they don't move anything before we've secured the data. Winger and Split Screen will coordinate on the audio side. Any questions?"

The line was silent for a few moments before Lorenzo continued. "Good. I'll work closely with Ghostlight, but I'm available if needed. Doctor Possible out."

The call terminated.

There was a sharp knock on the door, and John answered. He accepted a box. The electronics had arrived!

"Is there a plan?" he asked as he handed the box over.

I turned to the desk and looked for something to open the box with. I wanted to get the new laptop online to make this go faster.

I briefed John while I tore into the box.

He nodded and checked his phone. "Your parents need to see me, so I'll head back up. Where do you want to work from?"

I considered the options and the best choice was to stay next to this computer since control of the distribution system originated from it.

"I'll stay here."

I handed John the phone that had been in the box.

"Thanks." He powered on the device. "As soon as it's online, I'll be on comms."

I nodded as I turned on the new laptop.

"I'll get on comms too. I'll be on channel but also working with others to get this stopped."

"Sounds good. Stay safe." John held out his fist and we bumped with the explosion follow-up. I didn't know a fist bump could be somber, but we'd just managed one.

He left, and I got to work. As soon as I had the comm device in my ear, I got on with Split Screen.

She'd done impressive work. She'd tried to make it seem as though the signal was getting out, but instead blocked it at the source. She described it like a deception from spy movies where a mirror made a laser bounce back to its source so an alarm wouldn't be tripped.

As we talked about the issues she had with the execution, I reviewed the code. The reputation she'd gained in her short time with TOS was spot-on. She was great under pressure too.

"What if I write—" There was a crash outside the door. "Stand by. Something's happening here."

More sounds of struggle came from outside. I jumped from the chair to lock the door even though that would only buy me a few seconds.

"Winger, what is it?" Split Screen asked, urgency in her voice.

"Shotgun, are you on channel?"

Nothing. He must still be waiting for his phone to configure.

The position of the furniture would provide some cover, though hiding wasn't really possible. The desk faced away from the window and toward the door. I'd be able to crouch at the side of the desk that was most in the corner.

"I believe my security's been breached. Notify Shotgun, Defender, or Snowbird and get them on channel."

"On it," Split Screen responded.

The doorknob rattled, just like in a horror movie.

A moment later the door began to splinter.

I made myself as small as I could next to the desk. Someone had a gun with a silencer. The slight sound a gun makes as it popped bullets drifted into the office as shrapnel came through the door. The chair, desk, and window spiderwebbed with cracks as they were hit.

"I'm about to be overrun." I spoke quietly, my voice

even. Perhaps this was getting to be too much of a common-place situation for me to be outright scared.

"Defender here. We're on the way."

Right on time, as usual.

With a couple of loud thunks against the door, it gave way. I remained hidden. Obviously, I couldn't get out of the room, but not revealing myself would buy time for Dad to arrive.

"I know you're in here, Theo."

Melissa?

Wow.

She had an excellently crafted cover. As head of security, we'd vetted her early on. Nothing suspicious surfaced in her review—just someone who worked hard to get where she was.

I stood, hands raised, not wanting to provoke her. "What're you doing?"

"I can't let you cause any more issues than you already have." She aimed her gun at my chest. "We hoped there was enough distraction with the kidnappings and Eddie but apparently not. So much the better. I'll be a hero for bringing you in. Then you'll have no choice but to work with us. I was surprised you weren't taken last night."

Last night? Did she get to Eddie while he was here yesterday to force him to do what he did? Or was Eddie a willing accomplice? Did I even have a cover anymore?

So many questions.

"You can't really think they're gonna let me walk out of here with you. Homeland Security and FBI are in the building."

"Please. Your parents aren't going to risk your life."

She was wrong about being expendable. I had been in the past, and I had no doubt the mission trumped my safety.

"Hang tight," Mom said, *"we heard that. We're on the floor."*

"My husband told me you were good," Melissa said. "I've seen that firsthand now. It's time for you to join us, especially if you want your parents and friends to survive."

She spoke as if she was stating a fact to an old friend. Strangely it didn't even sound like a threat.

I didn't see a way to end this. There was no good option available to disarm her. I hoped Mom, Dad, and John had a plan. I stepped farther out from the desk and moved toward her slowly, hands still up.

"Your husband?" I quickly cataloged the people I knew and couldn't imagine who she referred to.

"You would know him as Westside."

No way!

He'd said in Denver this wasn't over. Does all of this connect to that? Westside should be locked—

"Drop your weapon! Get your hands up. There's nowhere for you to go." It was Dad, both in my ear and in the hallway.

Melissa shrugged and shook her head with a disappointed look. "Guess we're not doing this the easy way. Believe me when I say this isn't over, Theo. Or would you prefer to be called Winger?"

My eyes darted around trying to find options.

She slowly raised her hands as if she was going to surrender. The gun was aimed at the ceiling. It was only then that I noticed her left hand was fisted. What did she have?

"Something's in her left hand!"

I charged her. Her hand flexed without opening.

Music blared out of speakers. It was loud. They must be all over the floor.

No!

I put my hands over my ears but couldn't block the sound. The sensation was more intense—not just an itch but more like an ice pick chipping away inside my head.

"Winger?" Mom asked.

"N-no." I struggled to speak.

I looked at Melissa as rage took over.

"What did you do?" I yelled.

Is this what it felt like for Bruce Banner when he Hulked out?

I charged after her.

"Winger? I'm trying to block with my code," said Split Screen.

Melissa underestimated my speed as I tackled her to the floor. She hit the ground with an "oof." She fought back and that just fueled my rage.

I punched at her. Some she deflected but others connected on her face and chest. She landed a couple of blows with the gun, but they weren't enough to knock me off her.

The comm channel was chaos. Gunfire sounded somewhere on the floor.

Someone pulled me violently to my feet and threw me into the hallway. I smashed into a cubicle wall that gave way with the impact. I slid to the floor as the wall panel ended up at an angle against a desk.

I bounced to my feet. Supercharged, I looked around. Mom, Dad, and John were in hand-to-hand combat with others. Melissa's allies or people affected by the music?

I didn't care.

"Take him!" Melissa yelled as she was pulled to her feet.

The man who'd helped her made a move, and we closed

on each other fast. Punches flew as soon as we were close enough.

I wanted her, though. She made this happen.

I bounced back and lashed out with a sweeping kick. While he blocked it, he went off balance leaving him open to a second kick. My foot connected with the side of his head, and he crumpled to the floor.

I turned toward Melissa.

She looked horrified.

"Winger, stop." Voices in the comm and shouts from around me mixed together. The music continued to be the loudest thing, though.

Melissa backed up as I moved toward her.

"I can put a stop to this." The cocky confidence was gone from her voice, but she tried to own the situation. She held up the small remote control. "All you have to do is come with me."

I punched at the cubicle walls to my right. If I didn't I'd go crazy. Each time I lashed out, the fire in me eased for a moment.

Only a dozen paces or so separated me from Melissa.

I wanted to hurt her.

She was responsible for what Eddie had done.

I charged.

Her eyes went wide.

She pulled down one of the cubicle walls, showing her strength again. It leaned against the wall as she backed up and pulled another down.

Viciously, I picked the wall up and shoved it aside, so I could get through.

She turned to run, and I took off after her. She made a right at the end of cubicles, but my way was blocked by another man who'd come from the left.

His gun was drawn, but he couldn't react before I plowed into him, crashing him into tall filing cabinets. He was dazed as breath rushed out of him. I slammed his gun hand into the steel drawers until he released the weapon. He cried out as I kicked his left knee, which caused him to drop to the floor.

The door to the stairs clicked shut as I looked down the hall after Melissa. I sprinted, and in the stairwell, she was already a floor below me.

"You should just stop where you are," I called out. "You can't outrun me."

The music stopped.

I fell as I tripped over my feet.

The impact of the concrete hurt bad.

I slammed into the wall on the landing between floors.

My energy was gone.

"Winger here." My voice barely came out as I struggled to breathe. "I'm in the stairwell. Incapacitated."

"Now you have no choice but to come with me." Melissa had crept back up the stairs.

A gunshot rang out and Melissa recoiled, grabbing her shoulder. She turned to run but was stopped by three people behind her.

A stampede sounded as several people came downstairs. John went by me, gun drawn. He stopped in front of Melissa. Dad stopped midway between John and me. Mom, meanwhile, kneeled at my side.

"I'm with Winger," she said. "We've apprehended Melissa. The music has stopped, but there are several injuries and possibly fatalities here."

"Yoshi here." I didn't know he was on the mission. He'd led the Denver tracker mission. "I was patched in to let you know that we've taken the base of operation in Philly. We *recovered personnel and equipment. Everything is offline. We don't know if they destroyed anything."*

"Ghostlight here. From our monitoring, there's no sign they moved the data again. We believe we captured all of it before the equipment went offline. We'll analyze the tech recovered as well as the data to make sure we've got everything."

At least the immediate threat was over. I struggled to adjust because I was not in a comfortable position. It was difficult. Thankfully Mom helped me.

"How bad is it?" I asked.

"I don't know," she said. "Several people are down on twelve. We don't know yet how many people were affected inside the building. We also don't know yet what happened outside."

I nodded and it took almost all my energy to do that.

TWENTY-THREE

SOME FORTY PEOPLE at Glenwood Music were hurt as a result of the music blast. Luckily there were no casualties—at least not yet. The guy I kicked in the head was in a coma, and the doctors weren't sure if he'd pull through. I'd hurt people during missions before but never that badly.

The kick and its impact replayed in my head. While I trained to defend myself and to go on the offensive if I had to—I'd never done it before. I had a pretty good idea how Amp felt when he thought he'd shot someone. I couldn't shake the queasiness that loomed in my gut.

Melissa was in custody as were others who'd worked with her. There were more than twenty apprehended in Philly as part of the joint operation TOS coordinated with Homeland and the FBI. TOS took the lead on interrogation since its operatives had the most intel on Blackbird.

Once I was able to function and reasonably sure I wouldn't be sick, I accompanied John to a building TOS operates out of in Manhattan. We watched Mom and Dad question Melissa on a closed-circuit video feed. It seemed more like a discussion than an interrogation even though the conversation was pointedly around Blackbird's objectives.

"Why the attempted kidnappings?" Mom asked.

Melissa chuckled. "You know us. We like chaos."

"But you were already embedded at Glenwood."

She looked incredulous.

"If you don't tell us," Dad leaned in, "we have people who'll stop at nothing to get the answers." I'd never seen Dad in this scary mode before. The edge in his voice made the hairs stand up on the back of my neck.

More laughter. How did she act like this? Dad seemed to have no impact on her at all. "You guys don't torture. The worst you'll do is keep me locked up, just like you've done with Westside."

"Torture?" I looked to John.

"If we don't get answers, it'll be difficult to prepare and defend against whatever comes next. Sometimes our hand is forced."

Torture wasn't something I thought the good guys did. I'd thought about this after the tracker case. I'd asked Mom and Dad after Denver if we were good. They'd said yes. But, of course, they would. I imagined if I asked Melissa the same question, she'd be able to justify that Blackbird was doing the right thing.

How did my parents live this life? Was there always some kind of threat? Do they have to balance—or even cross back and forth—the fine line between good and bad?

The door opened off-screen and someone I didn't recognize came in. She carried a messenger bag that she set down on the table as she took a seat next to Mom.

"This is Javelin. She'll take the interrogation from here."

Without another word Mom and Dad left. Javelin opened the bag she'd brought and pulled out a smaller case.

"I'll give you one chance to tell us why Blackbird undertook this operation."

"I'm sure you can do better than just asking the same question again." Melissa's smugness continued.

Mom and Dad came into the conference room. Dad went directly to the monitor and turned it off.

I looked between them wanting answers—if there were any to get.

"You don't need to watch this." Dad sat down next to me. "There are certain parts of the agency you've never been exposed to. And while you'll see the interrogation report, you don't need to see how it's obtained."

Was this above my security clearance? Or was Dad protecting his son from an ugly side of TOS?

I'd seen enough movies to know what was possible. Hell, it even cropped up in real life news how governments sometimes got information. I appreciated that I wouldn't have to watch, especially since I wasn't sure how I felt about someone being harmed in the quest for details. It seemed wrong. What Melissa had done, though, could justify getting tough—people were hurt, data was stolen, and a business took a major hit.

I honestly didn't know what to think. They'd come after me. They'd taken Eddie from me. Or maybe he'd been part of it all along and was never really mine. Maybe….

I stopped before I went too far down the rabbit hole of trying to sort out my feelings. There were too many. Life was much easier when I stayed behind a computer in my room.

I looked at Dad and nodded. It was simpler to leave it at that.

"I suppose I should get back to work," I said. "Ghost-light and I are coding a way to clean all the files that are compromised just in case people don't know they have them. We want people to know their music is safe."

My phone vibrated in my pocket, and I recognized the pattern as Mitch. We hadn't talked outside of a few texts since I'd been in New York. He was used to me not surfacing when I was deep in work. The phone buzzed twice more in rapid succession. He texted at a fast rate.

"It's been a long, crazy day," Mom said. "Are you sure you don't need more recovery time after that last blast of music and the fights?"

Usually I liked being treated as a colleague by them, but there was a lot of me that really wanted to be a kid. I appreciated she offered the out. I needed to finish the mission, though, so I could focus on the rest of the mess.

Now Mitch was calling. Maybe something was wrong.

"I should take this." I pulled the phone from my pocket. "It's Mitch and he's shifted from texting to calling."

"Of course," Dad said. "Should we go?"

"Nah. It's not like he's top-secret." I gave a weak smile in an attempt to lighten the mood.

"Hey, Mitch, what's up?" I hoped my voice sounded as if everything was totally fine.

"Hey, man. Sorry to bother you." He spoke superfast. "I know you're busy. I saw your parents on the TV today, which, was like... well that never happens. But, look. This may be nothing... I don't know."

"Mitch? What's going on? Are you okay?"

Mom, Dad, and John focused on me, and I shrugged. I hoped this wasn't another problem, but it wasn't like Mitch to stumble over words so much.

"Like I said it may be nothing." He paused again. "I was out doing some errands for Dad and ended up driving by Eddie's. There's a for sale sign in front. I... well... I looked through the front window. Man, their stuff's gone. He's still down there, right?"

The news was like a gut punch. Mitch talked, but I only heard bits and pieces of it. The Cochranes packed up and left. Just like that.

"Theo? Theo!"

"Sorry. I'm here. You said the house was empty?" I looked at Mom, trying to keep my shit together. The nausea from earlier roared back.

"Yeah. I rang the bell, and there was no answer. I texted Eddie to ask what was up. Maybe his parents moved somewhere else in the city. I mean people move, right? But the text message bounced as undeliverable. He's not even on Facebook anymore. Unless he's blocked me. He's with you, right?"

I'd managed to put off thinking about Eddie much over the past twelve hours, but this made it all too clear that there was something major going on.

I dropped my head. I couldn't look at my parents.

Had Blackbird taken Eddie's parents? Taken him? Maybe he was forced to protect them? If Mom and Dad were in trouble, I'd do whatever it took to save them.

The shakes vibrated me, and I clutched the phone tight so I wouldn't drop it.

I had no idea what to say because it wouldn't necessarily match whatever story we created.

"He's still here," I managed to say with an even voice. "I'm just about wrapped up with the work and—"

I hung up on Mitch. Hopefully he thought the call dropped. I turned it off so any call back would roll to voicemail. I released the phone. It bounced off the table and ended up on the floor. I held my head in my hands as a huge sob escaped.

The agent part of me hated the outburst, but nothing would keep it in. Few things were worse than what Eddie'd done.

My chest hurt—between the fights and the convulsions caused by the emotions.

Mom and Dad both put their hands on my back. Mom's smaller hand rubbed a circle while Dad offered a gentle squeeze on my shoulder. I wanted the comfort, but at the same time I didn't because it threatened to make it worse.

"What did Mitch say?" Dad asked.

"Can we not talk about this right now?"

"If this was just a breakup, then yes you'd have all the space you need. But you know it's more than that." Mom's agent voice was in full force.

"Of course, I know that." I strained to keep my voice in check and abruptly stood up from the table.

Yelling at them wouldn't help. "They're gone, okay? The Cochranes packed up. Mitch happened by the house today, and it was empty with a sign out front and everything."

A look went between them I'd never seen before.

"We know," Mom said quietly.

Like a hinge had broken, my mouth dropped open as my mind reeled.

"For how long?" I shouted through increasing sobs. "How could you keep—" A coughing fit made everything worse.

Mom reached out, but I dodged her.

I'd never done that before.

"How long?" I finally asked through ragged breaths.

"A few hours. Agents went to the house right after we reported what Eddie had done. It's unclear if the family's gone into hiding or if they were taken. It's been made to look like they never existed. Many—"

For hours? Did they think I couldn't handle the news? I'd rather hear it from them instead of being blindsided by Mitch.

He'd said Eddie's Facebook was gone. That meant much of our history was too. He posted far more than me. All those pictures....

Like that was the most important thing. My priorities were messed up.

"I need some air." I grabbed the phone from the floor and my backpack off the table. "I'll get back to the brownstone."

Before I got to the door, Dad gently grabbed my arm.

"Theo—"

"Please," I looked at the floor. This wasn't the right thing to do but I needed out. "I *really* have to go. I'll let Lorenzo know I'll be back online later."

Mom came to me, and I caught the look of sadness on John's face as he stood by the table.

"Don't." I stopped Mom before she said anything. "If I stay here, I'm going to explode. I need to be on my own, okay?" The struggle not to scream took a lot of energy. "Then I'll refocus and finish the job."

I didn't give them an opportunity to say anything else as I shrugged off Dad's hand and left.

TWENTY-FOUR

BEFORE I LEFT the security of the building, I called Lorenzo. He didn't ask any questions about the delay. Either my parents had texted him, or he knew I must've finally hit a wall.

Mitch had left a flurry of text messages and two voice-mails. I'd owe him a huge apology later.

Outside the sun shone brightly in the western part of the sky, but it'd still be some time before it got dark.

I stood on the corner of Seventh Avenue and Twenty-Fourth Street. I knew from my basic Manhattan geography that I was pretty close to the Hudson River. Eddie and I wanted to rent bikes and ride along the waterfront since it stretched more than one hundred blocks. Down the street I saw bikes racked up outside a storefront. Maybe I could rent one. A ride would be perfect despite how tired I felt.

The bikes were outside a very nice bike shop—it reminded me of the one I frequented in Boston. Inside bikes, mostly mid- and high-end models, sat on display along with all sorts of accessories. In the back, someone worked on a bike in a repair area.

"Can I help you?" a young woman asked. She stood behind a counter along the right wall and wore shorts and a Bicycle Habitat T-shirt.

"Do you rent bikes?"

"We have some hourly rentals. Unfortunately, we stop renting at six on weekdays."

I nodded and looked around the store. Hanging on the wall was the same bike I had back home, except it was the newer model. I really wanted to ride. It would help so much more than a walk, run, or skate.

"How much is that bike?" I pointed to the one I wanted. I liked the steel gray color of the body—much more stylish than the flat black I owned. The new bike wouldn't be as customized as I'd made mine over the years, but it would more than do.

"That one is twelve hundred dollars. I can show you some cheaper ones that are not as light but might be more in your budget."

"I'll take it. I'd also like to swap out the clipless pedals for regular ones since I don't have my cleats."

She looked a little dumbfounded that I just agreed to spend more than a thousand dollars.

"Uhm, okay. Let me go ahead and pull this down, and we'll see about getting it fitted for you."

The apprehension was clear, and I couldn't blame her for it.

"If it makes you feel better, you can run my credit card first. Just let me add the pedals, riding shorts, a helmet, and lights and you can total it up." I reached for my wallet and a relieved smile played over her face.

Once she ran the card and verified my ID she was in a much better mood and even tried to apologize for her hesitancy. I thanked her and told her not to worry about it. It wasn't the first time it'd happened.

"The bike Liam's working on is actually due out this evening I'm not sure we can get the pedals swapped." She had the pedals in her hands.

"If I can borrow tools, I can do it myself and the fitting as well."

"Well okay, then." It wasn't long before she came back with tools and helped keep the bike steady, so I could do the work since there wasn't another rack to use.

Some of the stress fell away as I did something completely unrelated to the day.

I had the bike ready to go in no time. Because I serviced mine, making the adjustments was easy. I slipped into a changing room, so I could get into the bike shorts. Once that was done and I had my other shorts and the spare pedals in my pack, I was ready to go.

Riding west on Twenty-Third Street felt good as I could focus on the rhythm of pedaling. Riding alongside the evening traffic was the best thing I'd done since—well, since the run with Eddie in the park.

As I approached the western side of the city, the river came into view. I liked rivers. I routinely biked over them in Boston and, if I had time, I'd stop and just watch.

The park was beautiful—green grass areas, paths zigzagging through, and plenty of benches and some artwork. Not to mention the beautiful river that separated the city from New Jersey. Ferries and even a barge traveled on the water.

I dismounted the bike and walked around the grass, keeping to the pedestrian paths to get to the railing along the riverfront.

Eddie would like it here.

Where was he now? Still in the city? Back in Boston? Was he even in the country?

Was he safe?

Did he miss me like I missed him?

I squeezed my eyes shut to keep the tears in. I missed him. I shouldn't but I couldn't help it. We had plans—lots of them—and he'd vaporized them. I wanted to scream at him... and hug him. It was messed up.

So many questions that I'd probably never have answers to. Even if the Cochranes were found, how much would I get to know? My parents already kept details from me.

How had I missed what he was up to? More importantly, how was I found out? I always took steps to safeguard my TOS connections.

Nothing seemed amiss in our relationship. Eddie sometimes didn't like it when I got too busy and couldn't tell him exactly why, but over the last few months we'd worked through a lot of that. I'd even changed up how I worked to make sure there was more time for us.

While the relaxing vibe of the river washed over me, I did some of the exercises I got from Shields, to help still my mind. The problems didn't disappear, but it usually let me consider them in a more orderly fashion.

Shields sometimes seemed psychic with how easily she read me. Ridiculous, of course, since she was simply excellent at her job. However, the buzz in my pocket indicating her ringtone was still appropriate since I was employing her techniques.

As she identified, a barge horn sounded in the distance. "Where are you?" she asked.

"Standing in a park, watching the Hudson drift by."

"That sounds nice, especially after the day I've heard you've had."

I'd worked with her for several months now—ever since Denver. We talked once a week, and more if either one of us thought I needed it. I'd planned to call her later, but apparently she was alerted that I might need her sooner than that.

"I promise I was going to call." I shuffled through my pack for earbuds so I wouldn't have to hold the phone.

"People have been in touch with me so I thought I'd reach out."

"It's been...." I got the buds in my ears and considered what I wanted to say first. I didn't have to hold back with Shields, but where was the right place to start. Patient as always, she waited for me. "I thought Denver was about as bad as it could get. But.... I didn't know I could hurt like this."

My chest tightened. Despite the outburst I'd had earlier, I'd held a lot back and it roared in, filling me with so many feelings. I couldn't sort it out and didn't know how to explain it to Shields either.

"I don't know... How am I supposed to go forward?" Quickly realizing how that might sound, I clarified. "And I don't mean that in a suicidal way. But how do I work for TOS when I let myself get so compromised? And if I do, how do I get close to anybody again?"

"I'm glad you're not thinking of harming yourself—"

"Absolutely not," I emphasized.

"Good. Let's make sure it stays that way. Tell me, what's on your mind the most?"

"There's a battle for the top spot." I spoke softly so my voice wouldn't carry. Facing the river helped that as well. "I might have killed someone today and beyond that I *wanted* to hurt people. I couldn't stop myself. Then there's the situation with Eddie. How did that happen? I thought I knew him."

I thought I was done, but when Shields took in a breath to start her response, I stopped her.

"And please don't say most of this wasn't in my control. I get that. It doesn't change how bad this sucks."

"You got me," she said, a lightness in her voice that also soothed. "That's where I was going to start. I'm glad you already know that. Most of this will require time to get past. Talking will help so don't close yourself off. Honestly that's where the concern is right now."

A sigh escaped. "I probably shouldn't have taken off."

"Sounds like you relived some pressure, which is okay. People are worried because this is new for you."

"I'm not sure I can get used to this kind of thing."

"You don't want to get used to it. For most it's constantly learning how to manage the feelings that come. You've had multiple traumatic events in a short span, so your state of mind isn't a surprise. I'd be questioning you more if you were trying to push the weight of the incidents aside now that the mission is mostly complete. Honestly, you opening our conversation telling me how much you hurt was good."

I nodded.

"Winger?" she asked after I didn't speak.

"Sorry. I nodded and forgot to actually speak."

"How about this—hang out at the river, do what you need to do and call me later this evening? Whenever you're ready—whether it's five minutes from now or five hours. We'll dig into it all."

"That's a plan," I said. "Thanks."

"You should know that I have to report back that I've talked to you so people know you're safe."

"Of course. You can tell them I'll apologize later too."

So many people to apologize too—Mom and Dad, John, Lorenzo, the team.

"I'll do that. Talk to you soon, Winger." She disconnected.

I stayed where I was and watched boats travel the river for another hour or so. Once I was ready to go, I pulled up the GPS on my phone and saw the trip into Brooklyn would take about an hour.

No doubt the next few days—or maybe weeks—were going to be tough. The talk with Shields and the soothing water allowed me to get myself together so I wouldn't fly apart at the seams—at least for now.

I sent a group text to Mom, Dad, and John to let them know I was okay and biking back to Brooklyn. I didn't wait for a response. Since I didn't have a way to attach my phone to the handlebars, I set the GPS, left one earbud in—even though I hated biking with earbuds because it wasn't the safest thing—and rode out.

I kept a fairly slow pace, at least for me. The shared bike path had too many people, and I honestly wasn't in a hurry.

Sifting through my time with Eddie, so much awesome filled our time.

The first time I took him ice skating. He had such grace in the water when he swam but getting him used to skates? Such a mess. It took him a while to figure out his center of gravity and how it played into skating, and I enjoyed how he'd hang on to me to keep from falling.

He'd had a look of complete bliss when I introduced him to the peanut butter cream pie at Rose's. That was part of our second date after we saw some lame Zac Efron movie, which we only went to because he was shirtless in the previews. He'd never been to Rose's and it was one of my favorites. He loved the '50s retro tables and chairs along with the chili mac. The pie, though, had him moaning in delight, almost to an embarrassing degree.

Surprising me in Denver might be his best....

Denver.

He'd said he tagged along with his dad on a business trip, so he could see me play in the hockey tournament. Truth? Or did he know why I'd really made the trip?

Lorenzo had asked earlier this year—was someone using him to get to me?

There were events that didn't add up, especially around the computer science competition last year—the virus on his thumb drive, the weird signal from his home Wi-Fi, the odd time when my phone's security went off during our phone calls. It was easy to brush those away as coincidences.

Why would his family be involved in anything like that? Stupid question. I came from a family of covert agents. Why would mine be the only one?

And, Melissa's connection to Westside. Did we know he had a wife? None of that information made its way to me, but I wondered what TOS knew and if that threat had been on the radar.

What about Oliver too? This whole trip could've been an elaborate setup? It seemed unbelievable.

Unbelievable—a word that could be applied to so much after the past couple of days.

I focused on the ride going over the bridge and that cleared my head. As beautiful as the bridge was, it was a painful ride—and not in a good way. Forced to go too slow up the approach, to dodge and weave around the packs of oblivious pedestrians was frustrating. Once I was off the bridge I picked up speed to ride with traffic. The faster I went the better I felt.

The brownstone looked fully occupied when I arrived. Lights illuminated each floor, except for mine.

Once I let Mom and Dad know I'd arrived, a shower, more talk with Shields and work filled my evening to-do list. Thankfully everyone else left me alone.

TWENTY-FIVE

I woke up to my phone buzzing. Even before my eyes fully focused, I could tell it was pretty late because of the sun trying to eke its way through the closed curtains.

Yikes. The phone screen showed I'd slept past ten.

Granted I didn't go to bed until near three, but ten was still late because I could rarely sleep much past six.

"Hey, Mom," I said when I connected the call.

I remained lying in bed, sheet pulled up to my neck with just one arm out to hold the phone. I was sore. I enjoyed the good physical sore with my legs feeling like I might have overdone it. The headache was unfortunate.

"Sorry. I hoped I wouldn't wake you. Do you want to come for breakfast? We decided a home-cooked meal was in order."

I flashed back to when I was eight or nine and there'd always be breakfast on the weekends when Mom or Dad were home. Usually a big one with every type of breakfast food imaginable. As I got older, I helped with the prep. Sometime after I'd started with TOS, it kind of drifted away. I guess we all got too busy.

"I'd like that."

I could make a start of apologizing for yesterday too.

"Come on up. John's here too. We're just about to start cooking, so if you hurry you can get some of the first batch."

"I'll be there in a minute. Thanks, Mom."

"Love you, Theo."

I got up and shuffled into the bathroom. God, I looked awful. I could've done without seeing that. The dark circles under my eyes combined with the haggard expression represented the exhaustion that inhabited every part of me.

I splashed hot water across my face, hoping it would help.

It'd been a long night of work with Split Screen to finalize the code to clean the infected music. Some consumers would automatically get new files if they allowed Glenwood automatic updates. However, our program would also trigger a new file download if the device with an infected file connected to the internet in any way.

On the Glenwood Music side, the distribution system would go online today with clean files. I'd written a program to help make sure they only had clean files in the system.

I threw on shorts and a T-shirt from the clean stuff I had in the duffel bag before heading out. As soon as I walked into Mom and Dad's, I was hit with the smell of bacon and either pancakes or waffles.

"Wow, it smells good in here," I went straight to the kitchen area. "You might have the whole neighborhood here if that smell gets out."

"I'm really sorry I woke you." Mom left the stove where she'd been starting the bacon. She wrapped me in a hug that I held on to for a while. Once I let her go, she put a kiss on my forehead. "You're usually up so early, I figured you were down there working or even out riding."

"You can wake me up for breakfast anytime," I said as she went back to the stove. "It was a long night, but we got it done."

"Maybe you'll be able to take it easy today. I think we can all use a calm day," she said.

"Did you really buy a new bike?" John asked.

"Yeah. I really needed to be outside so I made an impulse buy." I looked around the small kitchen that seemed to have food prep going on atop every surface. "So, listen, I'm sorry about—"

"You were under a tremendous amount of stress." Dad sat the baking dish down that he'd pulled from a cupboard. "We owe you an apology too. We should've told you about the Cochrane's moving. You don't exactly need to be protected and it wasn't right you had to get that news from Mitch."

"I'll try not to yell at you guys again." I offered a weak smile.

"We'll try not to make it where you have to," Dad continued. Mom wrapped an arm around my back. "Especially for TOS related stuff."

Meaning if I messed up as a teenager, I'd still get an earful about it and be expected to take it.

"What can I do?" I looked around the kitchen, ready to move on.

"You want to take over pancakes or handle the eggs?" Dad asked, sounding relieved.

I raised an eyebrow at him. "You'd actually give me pancake detail? Seriously? You know my track record isn't pretty."

"Just giving you the choice of the available jobs." He smiled as he crossed the kitchen and ruffled my hair, which was still in full bed-head mode. The ruffle flashbacked again to breakfasts of childhood.

"I'll handle the scrambled eggs since it's hard to mess those up. When did all this food get here?"

"We went shopping earlier because we wanted the big breakfast," Mom said.

Was the need to cook for them or for me? I'd certainly been through the ringer. They had too, really. Hell, they probably had it worse since they juggled being agents and parents. Was that easier than what I did? I wasn't so sure since they had each other to worry about too.

As I drifted off to sleep last night, I tried to figure out the worst thing that had happened in the past nine months or so. Almost having Dad shoot me? Balancing student and agent during the computer science competition? Losing the rest of my junior year hockey season because I got shot?

And the latest—Eddie's double cross.

Individually, calling them horrible did seem to do them justice. Listed together, I didn't know how I avoided going off the deep end.

I had a great support system, though. Eddie had been a huge part of that, nesting in between my parents and Mitch.

Eddie and I complemented each other perfectly. I could relax him when he stressed, and he did the same for me. That alone left a huge void in my life. How did I bounce back from that and everything else he was to me?

"What're you thinking about?" John asked. "Are you expecting more from that egg?"

Oh man. I hadn't realized I'd stopped in the middle of cracking an egg, holding an empty shell over the mixing bowl.

"Sorry. Got caught up in my head."

Dad stopped arranging biscuits in the pan and put his arm around my shoulders pulling me tight against him. "I'm not going to try to tell you how you're supposed to feel, other than to let you know that you can do whatever you need to. We can talk about it or not. As a family, we love you, and that will never change. As your colleagues, you've done good work as always. This time it's been particularly hard, but you got the job done."

It was good to hear that. I felt like I'd really screwed up the mission side of it, though.

"Thanks." I didn't know what else to say. I hugged him back with an arm around his back.

There would be a lot of questions about Eddie and the Cochranes. In particular there'd be a search for any signs that something was amiss. TOS would have to figure out how they escaped all the checks that were supposed to be in place.

For me, it was a toss-up which discussion was going to be worse—talking with the agency or my friends. At least it was summertime so I wouldn't have to go back to school for several weeks. There was still Mitch and Iris.

Dad squeezed my shoulders again before he stepped back. I appreciated the support along with the fact that they were letting me decide what to talk about. I'm sure they knew from Shields that she and I had a long talk last night. She wouldn't have gone into details but it was a safe bet they at least knew she thought my overall mental health was as okay as it could be.

Comfortable silence hung in the air for a few moments while the breakfast tasks held our focus. This kitchen was smaller and laid out differently than ours, but we did a pretty good job of not running into each other.

Quite a feast ended up on the table. The kitchen counters became the serving space so the table wouldn't get over-crowded.

"So, we're pretty much done with what we came here to do," Mom said as we sat down with our plates. "We've got more debriefing to do with Oliver and his family, but that will probably finish today."

"We thought we could stay another day or two for some time off." Dad threw out the suggestion. "Oliver says we can stay as long as we want."

New York for a few days wouldn't be a bad thing. I didn't exactly have a need to rush home anymore. Having more time to figure out what the hell I'm telling people would be good too.

"I'm game."

"Anything in particular you'd like to do?" Mom asked.

"I have no idea. I didn't consider we'd be here to do vacation things. I'd love to bike around the city more."

"Let's all think about it," Dad said between forkfuls of food.

My phone vibrated with Lorenzo's pattern. "I should get this." I got up from the table and went to the living room.

As soon as I connected, Lorenzo gave his ID.

"How're you feeling, Winger?" he said. "I know it was rough yesterday."

He was such a good boss—usually taking that moment to ask how I was, especially after difficult missions. He took care of his people.

"Okay. Having breakfast with the family, so that's nice. Any word on how the program Split Screen and I worked on is doing in the field? I haven't had a chance to look at reports yet."

"It's only been a few hours but thousands of files have been cleaned. It's a great start."

"Have to say I enjoyed working with her. Her insights and skill in designing a fix were great. I'd love to do more with her."

"Good to hear. We were lucky to find her. She's already told me she liked pairing up with you. Teaming you two for some brainstorming on new initiatives could be very good."

After all of this, it'd be great to focus on work like that—back to the old days when I'd first started with the agency.

"That sounds great."

"Cool. We'll talk more about that when you get back to Boston." He paused, and I had a sense we were headed for topics neither of us wanted to talk about. "I wanted to bring you up-to-date about Eddie and his family. We still have no idea where they are. We're running all kinds of facial recognition and other protocols to try to determine where they've gone. Not only did Eddie's Facebook page disappear, but they've scrubbed everything else possible—DMV, personnel files from where his mom and dad worked, Eddie's school records. Taking out things like school records raises more questions than I'd want if I were disappearing. I'm sure they did what they felt they needed to."

How long had they planned their exit? Eliminating that much data took some orchestration.

If Eddie knew he was about to crush me when we were watching *Stranger Things* that night before I left, he'd hidden it perfectly. I shuddered a bit recalling hiding my face against him when I got scared. And later there'd been the bit of pillow fight and wrestling.

I sighed far louder than I meant to.

"Winger?"

"Sorry." I shook my head vigorously trying to clear it.

"They had a solid story to begin with. TOS ran the checks when I first met him and everything was right."

"That's the scary thing. They either fooled everyone and they were Blackbird agents right under our nose. Or, someone got to them and we missed it." Lorenzo paused for a moment, but I had no idea what to say. "Hopefully we'll find answers for you and us. There's a team devoted to this. Once I have anything I can share I'll let you know."

I ran my hand through my hair. Anything he *can* share. Made it sound like he might know something already. I wouldn't force him to tell me that I didn't have clearance. "If I can help let me know. And if I think of how to find them I'll definitely pass it along."

"I appreciate that. It's probably better if we don't involve you too much if for no other reason than it won't be easy for you."

"Understood."

"When are you headed back?" he asked, sounding more like his usual easygoing self. "It'll be nice to get you back to our planned projects."

"We're staying here for a couple of days. Decompress a bit. You know how I am, though. I don't do idle particularly well so I suspect I'll work at least a little."

"Winger, you're allowed time off. We'll schedule the overall debrief for next week and work on the lenses can pick up then too. You've given us so much data in the past few days that it'll be some time before we know what software adjustments need to be made."

"I appreciate that."

"I'll let you get back to breakfast. I'll update you if I get anything relevant. For now, though, consider yourself on vacation."

"Will do. Thanks, Doc."

"Take care, Winger. And if you need to talk, officially or unofficially, I'm here." He disconnected, and I pocketed the phone.

Returning to the table, I got questioning looks from the three of them.

"Just general updates, nothing too interesting."

Except it was all interesting. A struggle with myself brewed. I hated unsolved issues and Eddie was a huge one. It'd be too easy to focus on finding him. TOS didn't want me doing that. I knew it wasn't a good idea for me to dwell on it. Relaxing in the city would either be good to distract me or the worst thing. I'd talk to Shields about it. I had to make sure I didn't fall down that hole because nothing good would come from it.

TWENTY-SIX

I'D TAKEN a few hours to go out and explore Brooklyn, mostly just meandering around, but ultimately I rode along the coastline to Coney Island and the beach. I couldn't ask for a better day for a long ride—clear sky, mild temperature, slight breeze. I focused on my surroundings and how it felt to ride, keeping away from the noise that could easily take over.

Sofia was on the stoop as I arrived at the brownstone. Did she do this often? Maybe since this was where she grew up, she didn't have to worry about people bothering her. I was sure security was close at hand if anything did happen. She looked up from a notebook as I brought my bike up on the sidewalk.

"Hey." She sounded thoughtful as she closed the book. This was the Sofia I enjoyed most, when she seemed like regular people.

"What's up?" I leaned my bike against the railing that ran between the two buildings' staircases. "Working on new songs?"

"Yeah. I've got some ideas I want to show my dad.

Maybe we can work together more. The last few days have made me appreciate family all the more. It'd be crazy for me not to write with him after how good that first song was."

"Cool. I'd love to hear what you two can come up with."

We traded brief smiles. She looked like she had more on her mind. She needed to come out with it because I wasn't in the mood to fish for details with someone I hardly knew.

While I waited, I pulled a rag from my back pocket. I'd gotten it from the household staff before I'd left, to make sure I could clean up the bike. I loved the new wheels. I'd debated leaving it here, maybe donate or something. But it was too good to give up. I'd get in touch with the bike shop to see if they could break it down for shipping.

"Look, Theo, I'm sorry." She came down and stood over me as I crouched to wipe down the chain gears. "I don't know all the details, but I'm sure you and Eddie would still be together if I hadn't brought him here. It seemed like a cool idea to have your man around while you worked.... I should've left it alone."

I looked up at her, but when I couldn't figure out what to say, I focused on the bike. Sofia didn't move away.

"If there's anything I can do to make it up to you or fix it...."

I shook my head as I stood. "I don't think it can be fixed. I'm pretty sure this would've happened sooner or later. I suppose sooner was better."

She looked unsure and maybe a little sad. I put my hand on her shoulder, hoping to offer a little bit of comfort because this wasn't her fault.

"If you're sure." I dropped my hand, and she started to turn but stopped and fixed her dark brown eyes on me. "You're a good guy, Theo. I hope I find someone like you one day. And I'm sure you'll find someone worthy of you too. I know you've heard this from my folks, but thanks for the help. I don't know what would've happened without you guys."

"Thanks. I appreciate that." Unexpectedly she hugged me. It was the hug of a friend. Maybe we'd be that after I left. We certainly bonded over some weird stuff. "You going to be at the dinner tonight?"

"Wouldn't miss it. All of this has really taught me to hang with my family more. It's why I want to do a project with Dad. You're tight with your mom and dad. You even seem to enjoy working together. Anyway, I've always respected my parents. Appreciated what they built and what they do. But it's more than that with yours, and I'd like to get that with mine." She blushed a little and cast her gaze to the sidewalk for a moment. "I must sound silly."

"Not at all. It's good there are positive things coming out of the past few days."

"Well, I'll let you get back to your afternoon. I heard you're around for another day, so if you want to hang, I'm here. You're welcome to come to the Christmas show taping too."

"Thanks. Maybe. I'll let you know."

I couldn't imagine going to the show. Eddie'd been too excited for it.

My Eddie anyway. I didn't know the other Eddie—the one that had stolen mine. The one that could bring me dinner in one moment and then drug and steal from me was a stranger. I didn't want to know him. The idea of two Eddie's, while logically ridiculous, made things easier for the part of me that wanted to believe that at some point he'd actually loved me.

Sofia headed upstairs, and I grabbed my bike and went into my apartment.

Funny.

My apartment.

I sometimes called my bedroom my office. This, however, was by no stretch mine. It would've been better had I actually stayed upstairs with Mom and Dad because then Eddie couldn't have pulled off what he did.

How had Eddie let himself vanish? Could I do that? I couldn't imagine leaving Mitch, Iris, my friends, and everyone else without being able to contact them again.

Eddie had, either voluntarily or involuntarily, cut himself off from everyone.

TOS searched far and wide to find him. Maybe I could. What would it mean if I did?

As I'd done with my parents' phones years ago, I had planted a piece of code on Eddie's that I could track him with. I'd only used Dad's once—when he was missing in Denver. That was still something I'd never revealed to TOS or my parents.

I'd added it to Eddie's phone right after our one-year anniversary. I reasoned that he was family. The code was fairly impervious to wipe out or discovery because I put it in the root of the phone so even OS updates couldn't touch it.

Did I want to violate the rule I'd set for myself about not wanting to find him?

If I did, then what? We might get more information about his family's involvement. Of course, if I did that I'd have to admit how I did it. That might lead to the code I had on my parent's phones, and I didn't want that.

I dropped into the chair at the dining room table.

The laptop was right in front of me. I should just do it. If there was no blip, I wouldn't have to make a choice. If there was a blip at least I'd know, and then I could decide what to do.

I pulled the computer to me and went for it. I stayed incognito as much as possible so no one would know I'd done this if they examined the computer.

There was nothing.

That could mean anything—his phone could be turned off, destroyed, someone could've figured out how to get my code off it and he's walking around with the same Galaxy he's always had.

I slammed the laptop shut.

Why was I doing this? It wouldn't fix anything. Knowing if he was out there wouldn't give me my boyfriend back or even resolve the situation. It might look good as an agent if I brought him in.

It might also be better if I never knew if he was caught.

Eddie could be on the other side of the world. Depending on how much Blackbird wanted to hide him, he could even be disguised.

This morning Lorenzo had emailed me info. After Eddie left the apartment he walked to Grand Army Plaza and got on the Manhattan-bound 2 train. The last time any camera saw him was at Canal Street. He didn't get off the train, but a camera picked him up moving aside to let someone off. He was on the train when it left that station, but he was never seen on another camera. My phone was found on the train, inside one of the conductor compartments, later that night.

Lorenzo buzzed my phone, and it scared me. Did he know what I'd done? He couldn't have.

I plugged my earbuds in and connected.

"Glad I caught you." His word choice—*caught*—sent a shiver through me. "I know you're on break, but I'd really like your thoughts on something. We got the analysis back on the sound encoded in the song file. I wanted to see if you see the same thing I do."

"Of course. I'll look." I reopened the laptop and logged in to TOS.

The screen filled with code as soon as I was in.

"Do you want to tell me what I'm looking for, or would that be a spoiler?" I asked as I skimmed what he sent.

"I'd like to give you a moment. I want to make sure I'm not projecting something else onto it."

"Fair enough. I do like a challenge."

Lorenzo was quiet as I reviewed. It was only a couple of minutes before I saw similarities from.... Where had I seen this before?

Light bulbs went on. I went to another area on the TOS network to look over some analysis I'd done after we'd wrapped up the tracker project in Denver. I paged quickly through the report looking for what I wanted.

Lorenzo's call made perfect sense.

"There's code here that looks derivative of the mind control that we saw in the old tracker chips," I finally said. "Except in this case you don't need a chip implanted, you simply need to be someone able to hear the tone."

"Part of me hoped I was wrong because that's scary. I mean it doesn't mind control you per se, but the rage is potentially worse."

"We should run distinct analysis between the two and see where the similarities are."

"Can you imagine if Blackbird further refines this?" Lorenzo asked. He didn't need to say the rest. If they figured out how to do mind control simply through sound, the results would be horrible.

This triggered something else. "Remember the virus I found on Eddie's thumb drive?"

I displayed information back to Lorenzo. It was the disc image that my computer captured when the security alert happened. Most of it looked like schoolwork—a lot of Word docs, some spreadsheets and images. There were also sound files, which I had ignored at the time because I was focused on the actual virus.

Some of the files were labeled as class notes because Eddie liked to record some of his classes. There were others that appeared to be songs.

"Do you suppose some of those contain a version of what we've seen the past few days? This one's really interesting." I used the mouse to point at a file that was labeled as an Alicia Keys song but was a WAV file instead of an M4A. "Who uses WAV files for music anymore?"

"We'll get all of this looked at."

"You made a great find with that mind control stuff," I said.

"You too. You made the additional connections. Don't second-guess yourself, Winger. You're good at this."

I nodded, even though no one could see it. "Maybe they really were targeting me. Using Eddie. Maybe he's being forced."

"Maybe." Lorenzo's voice was quiet and reserved. "Thanks for taking a few minutes."

Not offering a theory was rare for Lorenzo. I'd left the door open to get more than *maybe*. It wouldn't be fair to push him to say more. The non-answer didn't help the ping-pong game that played in my head—Eddie betrayed me and needs to be captured versus Eddie was forced and I can rescue him. Running my hand through my hair, and massaging my head at least felt good even if it didn't quell the thoughts.

"For you, anytime," I said without missing a beat. "Call

me if anything else comes up. Tonight, it's dinner with family and the Glenwoods so I'll be able to slip away."

"Spend the time with your family. I'll only interrupt if it's urgent. Thanks, Winger."

"Talk soon, Doc."

I sat for a few minutes, computer still open. The screen cleared as Lorenzo disconnected. Thoughts raced around my head, slamming into my brain's virtual walls. The calm I'd found during the bike ride gone.

There was nothing more I could do for now.

A long shower was in order as was some aspirin for the headache that formed behind my eyes. Then it'd be time for dinner.

The Glenwoods planned to cook so everyone was involved, kinda like the breakfast I'd had yesterday. I expected tonight to be enjoyable and that the conversation would likely stay away from the mess of previous days.

TWENTY-SEVEN

Instead of flying home from New York, we headed to TOS HQ outside of Washington, DC. All of us had been called in to debrief. The last of the meetings took place in a conference room with Lorenzo, Joanna, who was his boss, and Raptor.

So far most of the questions revolved around why Mom and Dad started working with the Glenwoods without notifying TOS. While it was okay to help a friend, had TOS been aware of the details when they started, the response could've been faster once it was clear the agency needed to be fully engaged.

My interest piqued as the meeting shifted to details on the people taken into custody.

Raptor laid out the facts. "This is part of a Blackbird plan to cause extreme discord around the world. They went after Glenwood Music first because they're a smaller distributor. The plan was to roll this out across all types of audio, recorded and live, and be able to cause a segment of people to go berserk on a whim. They'd be able to have pop-up riots, on a global scale, whenever they wanted. We expect they'll continue to try and perfect this and make it so it can affect more people. It's a priority for Joanna, Lorenzo, and the tech teams to find a way to prevent this on a permanent basis."

The implications of Blackbird's plan where horrific. I imagined I'd be on the team—if I still had a job when this was done.

"We recovered everything in Philly," Raptor continued. "But, we have to assume they have as sophisticated of a backup system as we've got, and they're development work continues. We continue to question the people in our custody for information on the mastermind. We still don't know if Overture remains embedded with Blackbird as we haven't heard from him since his transmission was halted a few days ago."

In the years I've worked with TOS, I'd never seen Raptor hesitate. This was the guy no one knew by anything other than his codename. Always calm, cool, collected. The look that played across his face was unsettling.

"We also have to be aware that four, and possibly more, of our agents are compromised. In the coming days, we'll work with you together and separately to piece together how this could've happened so we can work to prevent it in the future. Our utmost concern now is for your safety."

Mom, Dad, and I discussed this before we'd left New York. We didn't include John because he'd have to decide how he wanted to proceed—stay with us or get a new assignment and identity.

We obviously wanted to be safe, and we talked a lot about the disruption of my final year in high school and my college plans.

"We've discussed this at length," Mom said, "and we'd

like to try to use this as an opportunity to make Blackbird fully reveal themselves. We can't speak for John and will respect whatever decision he makes, but for many reasons we'd like to stay where we are and continue in our present capacity."

Raptor nodded, but his concerned expression remained. "I respect and appreciate your decision, Victor, Katherine. I have to agree that using your blown cover in this way could be useful." He paused, and I fought to not squirm with the gaze he leveled at me. "But does that take into account what's best for Theo?"

"It's what I want too." At least my voice didn't betray my nerves since my insides felt like a knotted mess. "It's important to me because I feel I may have caused the breach." Raptor shook his head and waved his hand in front of his face. "I know we don't know for sure, and we may never know. But I want to help find closure on that and bring down Blackbird."

"I've been told a few times over the years that we forget you're not an adult because of your natural talent and adeptness in the job. But we cannot downplay the danger you're in. It's very important to the people at this table, that you in particular are good with what comes next."

That was another thing we talked about.

"I have a fairly good idea. There's a constant target on my back—on all of us really. Beyond seeing this through, I want to hang on to the day-to-day life I have."

Raptor looked to Joanna and Lorenzo. For the first time in years, I couldn't read Lorenzo's expression. He usually wore his feelings on the surface when he wasn't on a mission.

Would we be forced to relocate and change our identities or would TOS cut ties with us completely? Those options would be devastating, although in different ways. Moving would suck. Of course, being let go would suck too, especially for my parents. Even if it was *retirement*, I knew they weren't ready for that.

"And what about you, John?"

"I've been through too much with these guys to give it up. I'm staying put."

I'd hoped he would choose that because of the ties we have with him. I gave him a smile, which he returned.

"I can't say I'm not uneasy about the choice, but I admire everyone's desire to stay on the case and perhaps neutralize Blackbird once and for all."

Raptor stood and the rest of us did as well. He came around and shook hands with Dad. "Thank you all for your work." He moved on to Mom. "We'll keep fighting the good fight." He stopped when he got to me and, instead of the handshake, put his hand on my shoulders. "Theo, you make sure you take care of yourself." Then he shook my hand and gave me a clap on the shoulder.

"Yes, sir. Thank you."

"I have another meeting," Raptor said as he shook John's hand as well. "I'll leave you to finish up."

Once Raptor left, Lorenzo came around and put his arm across my shoulders. It was a very brotherly move. "Can I borrow Theo for a few minutes?"

"Of course," Mom said. "We have a few more things to do so you can take your time."

"Cool," he said and we exited. "Buy you a Dr Pepper?"

That put me at ease.

"I think we need to stop sending you in the field," he continued, dropping his arm so it was easier to walk. There was a lightness in his voice, and it left me unsure if he was joking or serious. "I feel like every time we do, something super bad happens."

Déjà vu swept over me and, as so many memories had done recently, clinched my heart. Mitch and Eddie had the same talk about me the last time we were all together. I stuffed the thoughts away quickly because this wasn't the place to dwell on them.

"You know, I've only officially done field work once. The computer science tournament and this didn't start as missions."

We arrived at the cafe, and Lorenzo pulled a Dr Pepper from the fridge and got himself a mineral water.

"Seriously? Water?"

He shrugged. "Yeah, trying to kick the soda habit. Girl-friend's idea. I'm not 100 percent sold on it."

I chuckled. Lorenzo had been with Ellen for about six months. He talked about her every now and then—just like I'd done with Eddie—when we goofed around playing video games.

"I'm not sure I could be with anybody who got between me and Dr Pepper." I held up the can before the full weight of what I'd just said crashed into me.

Sadness rolled in like cloud cover. I squeezed my eyes shut and rubbed them with my free hand. Lorenzo didn't need to see me cry. And it was stupid to cry over a soda or talking to Lorenzo about Ellen.

God.

"Sorry, I shouldn't of...." Lorenzo's hand was back on my shoulder with a squeeze.

"Don't worry about it. I've got to get used to it." I looked at him. "It's gonna be hell at home. I've only managed to put Mitch off by a few days since he thinks I detoured to work with a client. Times like this make me happy I'm almost never on Facebook because at least I'm not getting a million questions."

"I'm not sure I can say this enough—if there's anything I can do, or you want to talk. I'm here. As a friend or your boss. Whatever you need."

I opened the soda and took a long drink to buy me some time before I had to talk again.

"I appreciate that. I'll take you up on it if I need to." I looked at him sheepishly. "Can we talk about something else?"

We navigated the hallways to his office. "How was New York? The time-off part, I mean."

"I enjoyed biking around the city. It's different from Boston. And I had no idea how great the new bike would be. I can't wait to get it home. It was cool doing family tourist stuff too. We checked out the Statue of Liberty, went up the Empire State Building."

In his office we took our usual spots. Unsurprisingly nothing had changed here in the week or so since the training exercises.

"Can I be candid with you?"

Lorenzo usually spoke his mind, so the question was unexpected. "Always."

He hesitated, and I wished people would stop that. "After we finish working on the current prototype of the contacts, I want you to go on inactive status for the rest of the summer." I opened my mouth to protest, but he held up his hand, cutting me off. "This isn't a punishment, I promise. But you need time to work through what happened with Eddie. I know you blame yourself. And no, I don't know that because anyone has told me. I know because that's how you are."

He might as well have been striking me his words hit so

forcefully. I gripped the chair arms, feeling like I might either cry or throw up.

"And I see it in your eyes, right now. This is about keeping you in top shape. Everyone takes time off, and you don't take enough. You know how inactive works—we'll call you if we need to consult, but you won't be assigned a new project or mission until you're back."

I'd been on the vacation list from time to time—and even the injured and recovering list—but never inactive. People went inactive all the time for various reasons. I needed to buck up. Lorenzo of all people wouldn't do this if he didn't feel it was in everyone's best interest.

"Okay." I did my best to not sound disappointed. "You're probably right that it'll be good. As long as you're sure I'm not shirking my responsibilities."

"I would never think that of you. There are people twice your age who aren't as dedicated as you."

I nodded. I got my work ethic from years of being on hockey teams and from my parents. It was a good combo—watching them do their thing and playing sports with good coaches.

"I'm glad you're staying." Lorenzo sounded relieved. "I figured you'd want to, but this could've easily been the end too. We're gonna do everything we can to bring the Cochranes in and stop Blackbird."

"I know and I'll help where you want me to." Lorenzo nodded as I talked. "If you discover I compromised us please tell me."

"We will. It's important we figure it out and understand what we all missed. Security is reviewing all the protocols around identifying threats."

Lorenzo's video chat rang and he looked to his screen. "I

need to take this." His demeanor shifted as he pointed at the screen.

"Cool. I'll be back to work tomorrow."

He nodded. "Talk to you then. Later, man."

"See you."

I closed the door behind me as I left his office. At least the TOS side of life seemed sorted out.

TWENTY-EIGHT

ONE OF THE advantages to being on the high school hockey team was the ability to occasionally pick up free ice time and that's exactly what Mitch had pulled off for my first morning back.

We arrived just after six and played a version of one-on-one keep-away on a portion of the ice—blue line to goal line.

It was fast, intense, and a lot of fun. Since I'd been cleared for the ice again last spring, Mitch and I'd gone back to playing one-on-one a few times a month. We both enjoyed the challenge. I wished we could've played longer, but the summer youth camps had the ice next, so our time was up.

I dreaded the next part—breakfast. Despite the fact we always went to eat after one-on-one, this would be different. Mitch hadn't specifically said there'd be a talk, but we weren't going to sit across from each other and not end up on the subject of Eddie. Before I left New York, we'd talked because I had to apologize for hanging up on him. I told him Eddie and I had broken up but that it was too new to talk

227

about. He said all the right things a best friend would and let me be.

My parents had let me decide what the cover story would be. I ran it by them, of course. But they wanted me to be comfortable with it since I'd repeat it often.

Mitch, of course, was the best person to test it out on. We'd had each other's backs for forever, and he wouldn't push for more than I wanted to give.

We landed in our diner booth, which had been our go-to spot since back in our peewee divisions days when we'd come in, along with one parent or another, after Saturday morning games. The menu was huge, as were the portions.

This was more of a late-night place for us these days, usually with Iris and Eddie after whatever we did on weekends. Luckily there were plenty of memories here that predated Eddie by several years, so coming here didn't make me sad.

Once we ordered enough food to feed an army of hockey players, Mitch started with the simplest of questions.

"How are you?"

I shrugged and leaned back against the cushion, fiddling with the water glass in front of me. "I don't know. I mean I'm not dying or anything, but it's also like I've been pummeled. I didn't see it coming at all. I thought we'd talked about everything. We had plans. Hell, we'd fought last fall because he thought I was changing things when I went to that Denver tournament."

"Man, I thought he was better than that. Obviously, you knew him better, but we met him at the same time. I watched you two get all *cutesy*, as Iris once put it, but I never... I mean I don't know if you two were gonna be forever but... I never imagined he'd just cut ties because his parents moved to Vancouver."

I hadn't realized Mitch had thought so much about this. Although, possibly he was channeling Iris. I'm sure she had a lot of opinions. She told us once that she felt like we'd at least get through college together and believed we had a real shot to go on because we clicked so well.

She felt the same way about her and Mitch. Certainly among the people who have relationships at school, theirs was the one that always seems solid and the most drama free. Fights—and they didn't have many—settled quickly, and they never got bitchy with each other—at all. Eddie and I were the same—until we weren't.

"I can't figure out why he didn't think we'd be able to do long distance our senior year," I said. "We could've been back together for college. Parents sometimes move. But it doesn't mean you have to totally cut off the people around you."

"Did he...?" Mitch opted for a drink of water instead of finishing.

The server bought him more time by bringing drinks—coffee for Mitch and my Dr Pepper. Once we were alone again, Mitch seemed unsure and he folded the corner of the paper placemat.

"It's okay. Ask whatever."

Mitch was the only friend I'd give that permission to, but there was no reason for him to hold back. His sad expression was awful. It was opposite of Mitch's normal laid-back demeanor. Usually, the only exception was his laser-focused intensity for playing. The last time I remember him sad was right after one of his grandparents died when we were freshmen.

"Did he at least talk to you before he cut you out?"

"Yeah, broke up over dinner. He said he hated what he was doing, but thought it was best if he just walked away instead of trying long distance."

I kept it simple, and as close to the truth as I could.

"So that's it? We just don't see him or talk to him ever again? I'm still talking to some people that I went to grade school with, even though they've moved. I never expected him to be such a dick." He seemed like he was gonna say more but again stopped. "Sorry, it doesn't help if I badmouth him."

That coaxed a smile out of me. "It does a little bit. Believe me I've said lots of bad stuff about him in my head the past few days."

"Fair enough. Well, Iris wanted me to tell you that she's here for you just like I am. You probably already know that, but she wanted me to make sure. I'd told her she could come to breakfast, but she insisted this should just be us."

Iris was awesome. I would've been fine if she'd come, but I loved that she recognized the bond Mitch and I had. She'd get a big hug from me later.

Our food arrived, and it was slightly embarrassing that it took two servers to bring it all out.

"I know." I arranged plates in front of me. "You go to hockey camp in a couple of weeks, right?"

Mitch already had a mouthful of pancake, so he simply nodded and grunted an affirmative.

"You want some company?"

His face lit up like I'd given him a Christmas present. He chewed faster to clear his mouth, something Iris finally got him to do about a year ago after repeatedly punching him in the arm when he talked with food in his mouth.

"Hell yeah. It'd kick ass if you could come. I thought you had work?"

"I'm wrapping up a project and then I've got the rest of the summer off."

"That's awesome!" He said it way too loud causing other people to turn and look. He didn't seem to care and neither did I. "I'll send you the info so you can sign up. Last I heard there was still space, but they were filling up fast."

"Send it over and I'll take care of it today."

The camp was at Lake Placid, home of one of the best hockey games ever played. Going to camp with Mitch would be awesome and the perfect thing to do with your best friend before senior year started.

"We're gonna have a blast," he said.

"No doubt."

I GOT HOME to an empty house in the early afternoon. Mitch and I had an extremely long breakfast, and I suspected I wouldn't need to eat until at least dinner. Mom and Dad were actually out running errands as they didn't have a new assignment yet. John also took a few days off.

I headed upstairs to work on the project I'd promised to finish. There were code enhancements to make for some of the lenses' functionality, mostly around stability for the video when there was a lot of movement.

I worked until a notification flashed that the garage door was opening. Since my room was soundproofed for security purposes, I had set alerts for the garage, the doorbell and other things that might need attention.

I headed downstairs to see who was home.

Mom walked into the kitchen with groceries and mail in her hands.

"There's more bags in the trunk. Would you mind grabbing them?" she asked as she put down what she had on the counter.

"Sure thing."

I made quick work of bringing in the last three bags.

"Looks like you plan to be around for a while."

"Yeah. We decided to go inactive for a week."

I made a noise that was somewhere between a groan and a grunt. "You're not doing this because of me, are you?"

She paused putting away cans in the cupboard and looked at me with one of her patented Mom looks. "I won't even try to convince you otherwise. You can't expect us to push aside what happened to you."

I nodded and went over to her and gave her a hug, leaning my head against her shoulder. "I both love and hate that you're doing it."

She leaned her head against mine, and it was comforting.

"There's some mail for you," she said when we separated.

Snail mail for me? I preferred to keep communication electronic.

This was a small beige envelope about the size of a greeting card on top of other mail. For a second I thought maybe one of my grandparents had sent something.

The very neat block letter printing could only have come from one person, though.

"No way." The words escaped before I could stop them.

"What is it?" Mom came over to look.

I debated if I should just pocket it and play it off as nothing or share it. This would have to go to TOS for full analysis. The postmark was from somewhere I'd never heard of in Washington state.

A freak-out was distinctly possible. It felt like my heart was being squeezed. I sat down at the counter.

"It's from Eddie."

I gripped the sides of the envelope like it might try to fly away.

The garage door rumbled again. Dad was home.

"Are you sure?" Mom leaned in closer.

"I'd recognize this print anywhere."

"It's nice coming home to find everyone here," Dad said.

He sounded in a good mood. We watched as he put his messenger bag on the table.

I spun fully around on the stool and held up the letter. "Eddie sent this."

He joined us. "I don't even know what to say to that."

"We should treat this as evidence," Mom said. "I've got gloves here. We should protect it if you choose to open it."

She went to a kitchen drawer and pulled out some surgical gloves that we kept on hand for raw meat or hot peppers.

"I have to know." I put on the gloves, and Dad gave my shoulder a squeeze.

"We'll give you a minute," Mom said.

I nodded. I was more nervous than I'd been in a long time.

I got the paring knife and carefully sliced across the top of the envelope, making sure not to disturb the postmark. Did he pick out the stamp with the history of hockey on it? Was it a message? Or just the randomness of the post office?

The single piece of paper inside matched the envelope, and I was reminded again of my grandmothers who both had stationery sets. I couldn't imagine where Eddie would've picked this up. The note had the same print as the envelope.

I have no way to know if you'll actually read this. You might see the envelope, recognize the writing, and just turn it over to TOS.

Please know that I'm sorry. Everything got so complicated, but I had no choice. I know you understand that part. Orders are orders.

You weren't always a mission. We met and fell in love while I was a normal guy going to school. You'll always be the first boy I loved. And I'll always regret that we won't get to try for the future we'd planned.

I know you're trying to find me. And if you're not personally, TOS is. Please don't. Which I say knowing full well that someone will try even if it's not you.

I can't imagine how angry and hurt you are, and I hate that I did this to you. I hope you'll find a way to just remember me as your first love like you will always be for me.

Love always,

Eddie

There was no stopping the tears. They flowed on their own. At least I wasn't sobbing. I made sure not to drip on the letter.

I lived every day with the anger and hurt he mentioned. But, I couldn't deny he would always be the first boy I loved —and still did. I'd probably never forgive him, but I would always love what we'd had.

I folded the paper and slid it back into the envelope.

Grabbing a paper towel, I dabbed at my eyes, but the weeping continued.

My parents were in their office with the door open, so I went in. They were at their desks talking quietly, but they stopped as I approached.

"Please send this wherever it has to go." I placed the letter on the desk between them.

"You okay?"

I appreciated that Dad's first question wasn't about what the letter said.

The only thing that would've been more surprising than the letter would've been if he'd called.

"I guess. He said what he had to say. I don't have a way to respond, so it is what it is."

I dropped onto the couch opposite their desks. No one spoke for a few minutes. The letter must've surprised them as much as it did me.

"I want to go to hockey camp with Mitch if that's okay. I'll finish up the project with Lorenzo and then take his advice to go inactive."

As if it was choreographed, they got up together and came over. Dad took the opposite end of the couch, and Mom sat in the adjacent chair.

"That's a great idea," Mom said.

"Absolutely." Dad looked pleased.

"Thanks. It'll be awesome to get away with him."

"Let us know if you need us to do anything like sign paperwork," Mom said. "I'm so glad you decided to do this."

"Me too. There'll be enough breaks that I'll still be able to do what I committed to for Dr. Shorofsky so I'll be on track for MIT in the fall. We'll get back right before Labor Day."

Mom patted my hand and smiled more. She tried not to overdo the mom thing.

"I should get back to work." I also needed to think about the note.

"Okay. We'll be around. John's coming over tonight. We were thinking family movie night."

"Sounds great. That'll be nice. We haven't all done that in a long while."

I stood, hugged them both, and went back upstairs.

I'd already planned to cut back over the summer so Eddie and I could spend more time together. But now it was time to turn TOS off for a while.

Hockey camp would help put aside all things Eddie. Mitch wouldn't bring it up and no one there would know about it. Hockey and MIT research would make for a great month and the perfect remedy for everything that happened in New York.

ACKNOWLEDGEMENTS

Thank you for picking up Theo's third *Winger* adventure. As you may know, this series has a lot of pop culture influences behind it spanning several decades—titles like *Mr. Robot, Kingsman, Alias, Star Trek, Kim Possible,* and of course the everpresent 007 films. It's great fun paying homage to certain favorites as I write Theo's story.

Thanks to Michael for, once again, keeping an eye on what I had Theo doing in the drafts. Thanks to my husband, Will, for his tremendous support as well as the title of this book. *Audio Assault* was his idea, and I'm so happy he came up with it. Kudos also to the team that help made this book better in the editing process to ensure Theo's story is the best it can be: Dawn, Laura and Lee.

An extra special shout out to cover designer Aaron Anderson. If you look at the cover of *Tracker Hacker* you'll see a sort of electronic image over Theo's eye. I'd just started writing this book when I saw that cover and it immediately inspired a gadget for this book. Thanks, Aaron!

I mentioned the Ali Forney Center as the organization that honored Marcella. AFC is based in New York City with the mission "to protect LGBTQ youths from the harms of homelessness and empower them with the tools needed to live independently." They do incredible and important work. You can learn more about AFC, including how you can support them, at aliforneycenter.org.

I hope you're enjoying the series so far. You can tell me what you think at jeff@jeffadamswrites.com. I'd love to hear from you.

Theo's got one more mission to go. You'll see from the mission preview on the next page that the stakes are higher than ever...

MISSION PREVIEW

NETMINDER

CODENAME: WINGER #4

MISSION PREVIEW: NETMINDER

CHAPTER ONE

"Were we that awkward as freshmen?" I asked Mitch as we drove toward my house. While I usually biked home, after the long practice, I took Mitch up on the offer of a ride. Coach had worked the team extra hard in an effort to get the newbies into the right flow. "I don't remember being that slow or having Coach repeat himself so much."

"We were quick to catch on to the drills, but we didn't move very fast. It was a few games into the season before he actually put us in."

When practice had started two weeks ago, the returning team members reelected Mitch captain. He deserved the recognition for his sportsmanship, leadership, and stellar gameplay.

I was proud to see my best friend retain the title he deserved.

"Maybe I just want to remember the good stuff." I shot a grin his direction, which he must've seen from the corner of his eye since he smiled too. "Why did Coach pick players who can't follow instructions, though? Makes you wonder who tried out if these were the best choices."

"They'll catch on," Mitch said. "We're the seniors, so it's on us to set a good example so they'll improve like we did. And so they'll do it when it's their turn in four years."

We did have great seniors on the team when we were freshmen. Of course Mitch wanted to be the same for these guys. "I'm sure we'll do you proud."

"Please let me talk to Coach about making you the alternate? Alternate Captain Theo Reese has a great ring to it."

Mitch had pursued this relentlessly for days, even during our August hockey camp.

Camp had distracted me from what happened in New York earlier in the summer. Mitch and I had one conversation about it before the trip. After that I'd done my best to forget Eddie's betrayal, but I'd still lost it a few times. Mitch helped me dry my eyes and put myself back together. Thankfully he didn't push me to talk since I couldn't give more details than the flimsy cover story.

Weeks later I knew nothing about the TOS investigation into the Cochranes and the double-cross Eddie had pulled. It was outside my clearance, even though it had happened to me. If Mom and Dad knew anything—and they might not—they justifiably kept me in the dark. Meanwhile, the mess created by what Eddie did hit a new level of drama once I returned to school.

Eddie was a constant topic of discussion—both to my face and behind my back. Eddie had been responsible for most of my social media content because he'd tag me a lot. With his Facebook profile deleted and him gone from school, everyone wanted to know what was up.

I'd deliberately posted nothing. The rumor mill kicked in while Mitch and I were at camp, though, because he tagged me in camp pictures. The story became that I'd ditched Eddie to go with Mitch. Iris, Mitch's girlfriend, vigorously told commenters not to be stupid.

Iris was awesome that way. She also stayed away from the topic of where Eddie had gone.

The swim team questioned me relentlessly. Eddie was one of the stars, and they didn't appreciate my silence.

Everyone expected I'd have a story to tell.

Uncomfortable didn't begin to cover how I felt. I became more socially awkward than I could remember ever being because so many wanted to talk about *the* thing I didn't. I'd had no idea how much the school paid attention to our relationship.

Mitch stole glances at me. "You better tell me you're thinking about taking alternate. It's high time the team had one."

"Do you really think I'm a good choice when I'm already crazy busy?" I said, hoping to cover my Eddie spiral.

My watch pulsed with a notification, and I glanced at it. John went into my room.

Strange.

I couldn't remember a time that he'd entered my room without me at home. My security system's biometric door-knob would admit only four people—me, my parents, and John. What would he need in there?

I wasn't on a mission currently, focusing instead on upgrades to the ways agent phones and TOS apps inter-acted with Siri for voice commands. It was an easy way to get back into the swing of TOS after camp.

Mitch kept looking over, and I recognized the look. He was about to say something he thought I didn't want to hear. "Have you considered that you might work too much?" He capped the question with a smile.

"Yeah," I said with a groan attached. "Camp was epic and exactly the reset I needed. So, yeah, it's possible."

"Could I convince you to be alternate just by reminding you that I'm your captain?" Mitch pulled into the driveway alongside John's car. He put the car in park and gave me a stern look.

John and I had held down the home front for a week. Mom went to Portland to train agents on how to handle the effects of being deep undercover. Dad, meanwhile, continued on a mission somewhere in Europe. In an odd way it comforted me to know they were good going away at the same time since they'd watched over my emotional health so much, even after camp. It showed we'd all started to move pass the insanity of what had gone down before camp.

"Wouldn't it be an abuse of power?" It was an honor that he'd asked, but I didn't want to let him down if I had to put my attention elsewhere.

"All I'm doing is appealing to you as my friend, my teammate.... And someone who falls under my authority."

He tried to hold a serious face and failed, which ultimately cracked us both up.

"You need to work on that if you're going to try and influence people with that look." I smirked at him as I grabbed my pack and opened the door. "I'll see you in the morning. Thanks for the ride. Later, man."

We traded a fist bump before I closed the door. The hatch lifted as I came around to the back to unload my bike.

After gently pushing on the hatch so it'd close, I moved out of the way, so he could pull out. We traded a last wave as he passed.

I triggered the garage door with my phone.

Something felt off.

I racked the bike and gave it the usual end of day once-over but couldn't shake the odd feeling.

Nothing was out of place. Both cars were gone, and the stuff we stored—Christmas decorations, yard work tools, and random things in bins—looked undisturbed.

If I were Peter Parker, I'd say that my Spidey-sense was tingling.

My imagination must've gone off the rails. It had to be an overreaction to the notification about John going into my room.

In the kitchen the feeling intensified.

"John?" I called out as I grabbed a water from the fridge. No response.

The office door stood open. Anxiety spread, tightening my chest.

The room was empty, though there was a smell I couldn't place.

John's laptop stood open on his desk and his screensaver with the moving clock ran.

A photo on Dad's desk lay facedown. Weird. Maybe John had bumped the desk. I went to put it back in place.

I dropped the picture frame when I caught sight of his legs behind the desk. They were askew, one lying over the other.

"John!"

Had he collapsed?

I stopped short as I took in all of him. A pool of blood spread across his shirt.

That was the smell. I gagged, trying to keep from throwing up.

Shit.

His right hand was gone, blood spilled from his wrist. A cleaver lay next to him.

Jesus.

I stumbled backward, feet not working right.

Someone cut off his hand. He hadn't gone into my room at all....

The office spun, and I grabbed Dad's chair to steady myself. I couldn't pass out.

Was he dead?

I dropped my backpack and knelt next to him.

I should call.... Call who?

John was the one I called when shit went down, and my parents weren't home. We weren't supposed to call 911 for agents, but this....

I breathed through my mouth to minimize the smell.

The pulse in his uninjured wrist was barely there. His chest showed a very slight rise and fall.

"John!"

I flinched at the volume. There could still be people in the house. People in my room.

"John?" I was quieter and shook him gently.

First aid training didn't cover this. Maybe I could stop the bleeding. I needed something to tie off the arm. I unbuckled his belt, but it wouldn't slide out.

"Theo." He struggled to speak. His eyes barely fluttered open. "Run."

"But...."

"Run." His voice became crystal clear. "Now."

His hand clamped on my arm. I wanted to scream... or cry... or both.

"Go!" His eyes focused intensely on me for a couple of seconds and then shut.

His hand dropped.

Training kicked in. We had protocols for this.

When I was thirteen, Mom and Dad decided we

needed a plan "just in case." I never imagined we'd use it, not even after Eddie's betrayal.

I'd call 911 and TOS after I was gone. I hoped John could be saved.

John's instructions couldn't be ignored.

I grabbed my pack and ran upstairs, slowing when I saw my open door.

John's hand was on the floor.

Fuck.

I listened. No sound came from the room. I approached slowly, quietly, ready to defend myself.

Inside all the electronics were gone, including the stuff that was just for show. How'd they get it out without looking like a robbery?

I pulled my phone and it shook. I hadn't realized how I quaked.

It took longer than it should, but I sent the signal to fry the computers. I spared the phone and the laptop in my backpack, for now.

Frantically I threw stuff out of the closet—boxes of textbooks, my stash of Red Wings trading cards, spare computer parts, and other things I didn't use much. At least they hadn't been in here.

I removed a couple of the floor boards to reach my go stash—an unregistered phone, alternate ID, two thousand dollars cash, and some debit cards. I stuffed it all in one of the hidden compartments of my backpack.

The desk was a disaster with cables yanked from computers. Papers and knickknacks scattered across the surface and onto the floor. Drawers were pulled out too, and the contents were shuffled. They'd left behind what I wanted, though—the latest contact lens prototype. They were stored in a common lens case and that must've saved them.

My phone and watch beeped. The signal had gone out. Once any of my computers came online, they'd be toast. Between that and the security I had in place on the devices, no one should get anything sensitive.

The shakes intensified—adrenaline, shock, both. I almost dropped the phone.

I took a deep breath.

And another.

My voice had to be steady.

On the TOS phone, I placed an unsecured call to Mom.

She picked up after two rings. "Theo, what a nice surprise. You caught me getting some coffee between sessions. How was your day?"

"It was good." Thank God I had practice trying to sound calm when I was anything but. "We had a grueling practice trying to whip the freshmen into shape. And Mitch is still trying to convince me to be alternate."

"I think you'd be good at that. But I won't say more. I'll leave the persuading to him." She was proud he asked me, and she'd done some subtle campaigning for it. All part of me being a teenager as much as possible.

I took an extra deep breath.

"Yeah, he's really laying it on. Anyway, I wanted to let you know I'm going to Roger's house to work on a project."

Roger's house was the code we'd set up in case I was in danger and going into hiding.

"Okay. Tell Roger's mom I said hello." Another pause. No doubt she had the same struggle I did—what to say given the circumstances. "My break's wrapping up, so I need to get back. And you should go before it gets too dark." Always a mom.

"Thanks, Mom. I love you."

"Love you too, Theo." I heard the concern, the slightest fault in her voice. I doubted anyone who might be listening would register it. "See you in a few days."

We disconnected. I looked at the screen for just a moment before I pocketed the phone.

I had to go.

———

Winger's missions conclude with *Netminder*
Available in ebook, paperback and audiobook

This excerpt is Copyright © 2019 by Jeff Adams

YOUNG ADULT BOOKS BY JEFF ADAMS

Each of these titles are available in ebook, paperback and
audiobook

Codename: Winger series

Tracker Hacker (includes the bonus short story *A Very Winger
Christmas*)

Schooled

Audio Assault

Netminder

Other Young Adult Titles

Flipping for Him

ABOUT THE AUTHOR

Jeff Adams has written stories since he was in middle school and became a published author in 2009 when his first short stories were published. He writes both gay romance and LGBTQ+ young adult fiction...and there's usually a hockey player at the center of the story.

Jeff lives in central California with his husband of more than twenty years, Will. Some of his favorite things include the musicals *Rent* and *[title of show]*, the Detroit Red Wings and Pittsburgh Penguins hockey teams, and the reality TV competition *So You Think You Can Dance*. He, of course, loves to read, but there isn't enough space to list out his favorite books.

Jeff and Will are also podcasters. The *Big Gay Fiction Podcast* is a weekly show devoted to gay romance as well as pop culture. New episodes come out every Monday at BigGayFictionPodcast.com.

Learn more about Jeff, his books and find his social media links at JeffAdamsWrites.com.